He would be an exciting lover.

Alex sat on the edge of the bed and turned out the light, then dragged both hands through her tousled hair.

What was it about Grant Malone that had her reacting like a girl with her first crush? Even now, just thinking about the look in his eyes had her heart racing, her palms sweating. What in the world was happening to her? She wanted, right this minute, to have that muscled body pressed to hers.

Enough of this, she cautioned herself. The last thing she needed was to start entertaining any ideas about romancing a guest.

Alex lay down and snuggled under the blankets. From her stereo came the voice of Tony Bennett crooning about leaving his heart in San Francisco. She had no intention of leaving hers anywhere…or with anyone… except Grant Malone…

Dear Reader,

Welcome to Silhouette Sensation®—six fabulous novels of romantic suspense.

Hero at Large continues our A YEAR OF LOVING DANGEROUSLY series with another wonderful story featuring the agents of SPEAR. Then 36 HOURS continues with *A Thanksgiving To Remember* from Margaret Watson, where the mystery unravels a little more… The next book in this 36 HOURS set of stories is the Christmas anthology, *The Christmas That Changed Everything*.

Ruth Langan, an established historical star who you took to your hearts earlier in the year with THE WILDES OF WYOMING series, returns this month with the first in a new trilogy about the Sullivan sisters—*Awakening Alex*.

We're also thrilled to have three terrific stand-alone books: *Madigan's Wife* by Linda Winstead Jones, *Runaway Bridesmaid* by Karen Templeton and *Bluer Than Velvet* from Mary McBride. Irresistible!

Enjoy!

The Editors

PS New on the shelf this month are Silhouette Superromances—even longer, really exciting, deeply emotional stories. Perfect for those of you who like a more complex, bigger book—take a look!

Awakening Alex

RUTH LANGAN

SILHOUETTE
SENSATION

*First published in Great Britain 2001
Silhouette Books, Eton House, 18-24 Paradise Road,
Richmond, Surrey TW9 1SR*

© Ruth Ryan Langan 2001

ISBN 0 373 27124 7

18-1101

*Printed and bound in Spain
by Litografia Rosés S.A., Barcelona*

RUTH LANGAN

Award-winning and best-selling author Ruth Langan
creates characters that *Affaire de Coeur* magazine has
called 'so incredibly human, the reader will expect them
to come over for tea.' Four of Ruth's books have been
finalists for the Romance Writers of America's RITA
Award. Over the years, she has given dozens of print,
radio and TV interviews. Married to her childhood
sweetheart, she has raised five children and lives in
Michigan, the state where she was born and raised.

For Carol, whose heart is so open and generous.

And for Tom, our snug harbour.

Prologue

Snug Harbor Lodge—Snug Harbor,
New Hampshire—1980

"Grandpa Sully! Grandpa Sully! Hurry! Come quick!" The high-pitched sounds of two little girls shouting in excitement caused their grandfather to drop his fishing pole and scramble along the length of the dock until he reached them on a stretch of hill overlooking the lake.

His granddaughters, eight-year-old Lizbeth and seven-year-old Celeste were gathered around their nine-year-old sister, Alexandra, who was kneeling in the dirt.

"What's happened, lassie?" As always, when

he was agitated, Patrick Joseph Sullivan's Irish brogue thickened. He pushed his way between them and dropped to his knees beside the oldest of his granddaughters. "Did you fall, darlin'? Are you bleedin'?"

He'd seen Alexandra hiking the woods nearby, but he hadn't worried, since Buck Thornton, his lodge manager and trail guide, had been with her. Old Buck would never let anything happen to the dark-haired little girl who had become his shadow. From the first day she'd arrived at the lodge, Alex had been tagging along behind the grizzled old woodsman, asking a million questions.

Where do the animals sleep at night?

How do the squirrels know where they stored their nuts?

Why did the moss only grow on certain trees?

Were the stars always in the same place in the sky every night?

Since their arrival at Snug Harbor Lodge, Lizbeth, a plump, curly-haired urchin, had taken herself off to the garden to pass the days picking sweet ripe strawberries. Celeste, ever the little lady, preferred lying in a hammock and reading her books, her red hair and milk white skin carefully hidden from the sun. Only Alexandra had shown any interest in paddling a boat, hiking the nearby hills or swimming in the frigid lake.

"Alex found something in the woods." Lizbeth stared at her sister's cupped hands, eager to see.

"It's nothing but a filthy old bird," Celeste said, wrinkling her nose.

"Oh, Alex. You shouldn't have taken him from his nest," Lizbeth scolded.

"He's wounded, Grandpa Sully." Alexandra looked at her grandfather with brimming eyes. "His mother and the rest of the babies were all dead. Buck said, from the prints around the tree, it was probably a hungry raccoon."

"You've got bird blood on your hands. That's disgusting." Celeste flounced away, still wrinkling her nose.

"What're you going to do with him?" Lizbeth took a step back, hoping to avoid getting any stains on her tidy shorts.

"I want to help him. Can I, Grandpa Sully?"

Paddy Sullivan put a hand on his granddaughter's shoulder. "You can try, honey. But without his mother to feed him, he probably won't make it."

"That's what Buck said. But I want to try."

He nodded. "Okay, darlin'. You'll need to keep him warm. And then you'd better figure out how to find worms and grind them up so he can swallow them."

"Eeeyeou." Disgusted, Lizbeth ran off, leaving

Alexandra scrambling to her feet, stroking the tiny bird's head.

"Don't worry, little bird. I'll take care of you," she crooned as she headed toward the warmth of the fireplace inside the lodge. "I'll find you a cozy bed, and then I'll hunt you up a tasty dinner."

With a bemused expression Paddy Sullivan stood watching. His son and daughter-in-law often worried about their oldest daughter, who would rather play ice hockey than figure skate, and who preferred hiking and boating to ballet and tea parties. But he had no such concerns. She may be a tough little tomboy, but she had the most tender of all hearts.

He shook his head as he returned to the dock and tossed out his fishing line, hoping to hook enough bass for dinner. If anyone could nurse a wounded critter back to life, it would be his little Alex. In fact, he'd put his money on that tenacious little female to succeed at whatever she put her mind to.

Chapter 1

The long, drawn out wail of a tenor sax issued from the car radio. It was a sound that never failed to stir the senses. But Grant Malone tuned it out. The scenery of the New Hampshire countryside was postcard-perfect in the autumn sunshine, but he never even noticed. His thoughts had turned inward. Dark, tormented thoughts that blotted out whatever beauty there might be around him. His mind was filled with images of death and destruction. Twisted images from which he could find no relief. By day they stalked him. By night they crept into his dreams, so that even in sleep there was no refuge.

After leaving the little village of Snug Harbor,

he pulled off the road to study the map. A short time later he turned the Jeep onto a dirt trail and followed along a series of twists and turns until he spotted the rustic covered bridge up ahead. Starkly simple, its red roof glistened in the late afternoon sunshine. This, more than anything he'd encountered so far, had the look of New England about it. At some other time he might have admired the clever design that protected the wooden trusswork from rain, snow and ice. But his mind was far too distracted to appreciate the craftsman's handiwork.

As he emerged on the other end, a wooden sign confirmed that he was approaching the Snug Harbor Lodge. With a sigh he swerved up the rutted driveway until he came to a bumpy stop. He'd been on the road for more than ten hours, and his cramped muscles were beginning to protest.

He stepped out of the vehicle and rolled his shoulders, then looked up to see an old man just rounding the building. His hair was little more than tufts of white cotton, around a face the texture of leather, deeply tanned and marked with lines of age. He wore bib overalls over a plaid shirt with the sleeves rolled to his elbows. On his feet were sturdy boots.

"Afternoon." Grant's voice held the rough edge of tension. "Are you Alex?"

"Nope." The old man shifted a bucket of paint to his other hand before pointing. "Down there."

"Thanks." Grant slammed the door and started off toward the lake. The surrounding forest of evergreen and fiery maple, purple oak and yellow ash were a riot of color reflected in the water's glassy surface. It was more brilliant than any artist's canvas. But the beauty of the scene, like everything he'd witnessed so far this day, was lost on Grant.

Along the shore he spotted a line of canoes and rowboats, all overturned and resting on sawhorses. As he drew closer he could see someone in faded sweats and a baseball cap kneeling in the dirt, making long smooth strokes with a paintbrush.

"Hey."

A head came up at his shout. A hand paused in midstroke, then continued on until the last section was completed.

"You must be Alex," he called.

"That's right. Alexandra Sullivan." The voice was pure velvet. And the face, when she turned and he caught sight of it, was unmistakably female. And stunningly beautiful, despite the dab of paint on her nose.

At some other time he would have given a long, slow look of pure male appreciation. And then would have taken his time to bask in the glow of that smile. But that was before. Before his life had become a series of painful self-examinations and bitter bouts of self-doubt.

"Grant Malone." He extended his hand and

waited as she set down the paintbrush and wiped
her hand on a rag before accepting his handshake.

"Welcome to Snug Harbor Lodge. Any trouble
finding your way?"

"No. The map was pretty clear." His eyes narrowed as he peered around, assessing the terrain.
There were a hundred places where a gunman with
a high-powered rifle could conceal himself, if he
were so inclined. Grant felt entirely too vulnerable
standing here in the open. He much preferred the
danger of the familiar city to the unknown hazards
of this unfamiliar countryside.

What had ever possessed him to believe that he
could find some sort of solace out here in the middle of nowhere?

Misreading his tension as fatigue, Alex smiled,
hoping to put him at ease. "My grandfather said
you didn't know how long you'd be staying."

"That's right." He swung his gaze back to her.
There was no answering smile on his lips. "I was
told that wouldn't be a problem."

"I don't mind if you don't." She picked up the
paintbrush. "Stay as long as you want. But you'll
be roughing it. This is our off-season."

As the old man walked up to join them, she gave
a nod of her head. "Have you met Lem? Lem Lat-
imer, this is Grant Malone."

The two men shook hands.

Alex added, "Lem and I use this time to make

repairs to the lodge and equipment. That doesn't leave us much time to visit.''

Grant's tone hardened. ''I didn't come up here to be entertained.''

''That's good.'' The old man gave a terse laugh and glanced at Alex, who nodded.

''The only entertainment you'll see these days is provided by the wildlife. The deer have figured out that hunting season is over. They often come right up to the windows and peek inside.'' Alex chuckled. ''So don't worry if you see a set of antlers silhouetted against the shades some night. It's not a prowler. Just a curious deer.''

When there was no answering laugh from Grant Malone, she returned to her painting. ''You may as well settle in with your gear. Once inside the main room, hang a right and follow the hallway. It's the first bedroom on the left.''

''Thanks.'' He turned away.

As he made his way to the Jeep, Alex glanced up and studied his retreating figure. Seeing Lem watching her, she shot him a sideways look. ''Real friendly, isn't he?''

The old man gave one of his lopsided grins. ''Looks like he's got troubles.''

''Yeah. Don't we all?'' As she returned to her work she mused aloud, ''Funny. When my grandfather asked me to do a favor for an old friend, I just assumed he'd be...'' She shrugged. ''...old.''

"Maybe he's the son of an old friend."

"Must be." She forced her attention to the job at hand and gave a sigh. "Now I guess I'll have to give some thought to what I'll fix for supper."

"Thought you enjoyed cooking."

"I do. When we're out on the trail hunting and fishing. But this time of year, I look forward to a break from routine. I was already thinking about taking a long soak in the bathtub tonight, and maybe enjoying a grilled cheese sandwich in bed, along with a good book."

The old man gave a snort of laughter. "So hand him a grilled cheese and tell him he's on his own."

"I might do that." She bent to her work. "But I'll worry about it later. Right now I want to get these finished before dark."

Grant hauled his battered duffel from the back of the Jeep and made his way inside the lodge. In the great room he paused to look around. Hot coals from a wood fire glowed on the hearth. The fireplace was built of massive stones and soared all the way to the ceiling. Up above was the carved mahogany railing of a second-floor balcony that ringed the entire room. The ceiling revealed rough-hewn wooden beams.

He carried his bag down the hall and located his room. Inside was a king-size bed covered with a green plaid quilt and half a dozen plump pillows.

Across the room was a fireplace, already arranged with logs and kindling on the grate, and more logs stacked beside it. In front of the fireplace was a comfortable overstuffed chair and ottoman, as well as a side table with a reading lamp and a pile of books. Along another wall was a desk and chair, a television and stereo, and what appeared to be a well-stocked library of music and videos.

He unpacked, hanging his clothes in an armoire, before carrying his shaving kit to the bathroom. It had a separate dressing area, a shower big enough for two, and a whirlpool tub presumably needed to soothe muscles after a day of tramping through the woods.

Grant's frown grew. If this was roughing it, he'd hate to think what Alexandra Sullivan considered luxurious.

Alex. He stowed his shaving gear, before carrying the kit to the closet and depositing it in his empty suitcase. Not at all the type he'd expected to find running a sportsman's lodge.

Though his grandfather had often spoken about the Sullivan family, and the many hotels and inns they owned and operated, he'd never given Grant any reason to think the manager of Snug Harbor Lodge was a beautiful woman.

Not that it mattered. She could be as glamorous as a movie star and he still wouldn't be interested. What he craved, desperately, was time alone.

Time. He didn't think there was enough left to
heal the hole in his heart. But it was what all the
so-called experts had recommended. And since
nothing else had helped, he'd decided to give it a
try. He would kill time—an interesting choice of
words, he thought with a grimace—here in this
wilderness lodge, doing exactly as he pleased. He
could stay in bed all day, or read or do nothing
more challenging than lie on his back and watch
the shifting pattern of the clouds in the sky.

It would certainly be different, he thought. He
couldn't recall the last time he'd done absolutely
nothing. Probably not since he was a kid. And even
then he'd always been involved in a dozen different sports. Soccer, football, hockey, the skiing
team. Not to mention cross-country and swimming.
He'd always enjoyed the challenge of hard, physical sports.

He untied his trail boots and nudged them off,
then turned down the quilt and sat on the edge of
the bed. Pulling open the drawer of the night table,
he slipped his pistol from its shoulder holster and
dropped it inside, then closed the drawer and eased
back against the pillows. Within minutes he was
sound asleep. And once again facing the demons
that stalked him in his dreams.

"I'll take that." Lem took the paint can from
Alex's hand and started toward the maintenance
shed.

She picked up the paintbrushes and followed. Outside the shed the two worked in companionable silence, cleaning the brushes, using rags dipped in turpentine to remove the paint from their hands.

Alex glanced skyward. "If it doesn't rain tomorrow, we should finish with the boats."

"Won't rain." The old man touched a hand to his knee. "This old joint would know if rain was coming."

He opened the door of the shed and carefully put away the brushes and rags. It was a matter of pride to him that this workplace was as spotless as the grounds. He'd been seeing to the care of this lodge for more than fifty years. It was then that he'd erected a sign above the door, each letter carefully burned into the wood, that read A Place For Everything. Everything In Its Place. He not only approved that motto, he lived it.

"Good. I'll take your knee's word for it." Alex gave him a smile as she closed the shed door behind him and latched it. "See you tomorrow, Lem. Tell Marge I said hi."

"Yep." He headed toward his truck parked beside the Jeep. With his hand on the door, he turned. "If you change your mind about that grilled cheese, Marge said she was making venison stew. I could bring you some."

"Thanks, Lem, but that's too much trouble. Enjoy your evening, and I'll do the same. Right now all I can think about is a long hot bath. Good night.''

'''Night, Alex.'' He was whistling as he stepped into his truck.

She climbed the steps to the lodge and let herself in, then glanced around. In the growing twilight, her guest was nowhere to be seen.

She'd expected to find him sitting in front of a roaring fire, a drink in his hand. That was where most of the guests could be found unwinding after the long drive up here.

She tossed a log on the hot coals before heading off to her room. As she passed Grant's room, she noticed that the door was closed. There was no light coming from beneath it. It seemed awfully early to be asleep. But then, travel had a way of throwing a body off schedule.

She made her way to her own suite of rooms and began peeling off her clothes as she crossed to the bath. When the tub was filled, she turned on the jets and sank into the warm, swirling water with a sigh of pure satisfaction.

More than an hour later, her hair damp and curling from the steam, she slipped into fresh denims and a turtleneck and headed toward the kitchen.

As she passed Grant's room, she noted that the door was still closed.

She started to walk on when she heard a sound from within. Was that a moan? She turned back and pressed her ear to the door. She heard it again, only louder. Definitely a moan. Was he sick? In distress?

She turned the knob and pushed the door inward. Though the room was in darkness, the light from the hallway spilled inside, illuminating the figure in the bed. She hurried to his side and leaned down to touch his shoulder.

In the blink of an eye, everything changed.

Grant surfaced instantly. One minute he'd been locked in the throes of his nightmare, dueling with the demons from hell. The next he was aware of a figure leaning over him. His reaction was purely instinctive. Not knowing whether the hand beside his was holding a knife or a gun, he had but one choice.

His hand snaked out, closing around Alex's wrist with such strength she found herself pulled off her feet and sprawled across him on the bed. In a flash he rolled over, pinning her down on the mattress. In one smooth motion he had her two hands held firmly in one of his, and pulled roughly over her head. His other hand was at her throat.

His face, so close to hers, was a scowl of fury. "Who are you? What are you doing here?"

"I…" She couldn't think. Couldn't breathe. All the air had been knocked from her lungs. She'd been caught completely off guard. This wasn't at all what she'd been expecting.

Though slender, Alex was in excellent physical condition. From the time she was no more than a girl, she'd been hunting, fishing and backpacking in these forests. She could climb a mountain, row a boat or paddle a canoe while barely breaking a sweat. But all her strength was useless against the body that was pinning her to the bed. It was pure muscle and sinew. A lean, taut weapon honed to perfection. Capable of meting out physical punishment without flinching.

She struggled against the fingers still locked around her throat. And though they could have easily crushed her windpipe, they were simply holding her immobile. "I'm Alex." Her words were little more than a hoarse whisper. "Alexandra Sullivan. I heard a moan. I thought you might be sick. Or in trouble."

He heard the nerves in that sultry voice. Remorse washed over him.

"Sorry." In one smooth motion he released her and rolled from the bed. It occurred to Alex that he moved like a cat. Then he reached down and caught her hand, helping her to her feet. "You caught me in a dream."

"Some dream." As soon as she'd regained her footing she took a step back, away from the bed. **Away from this strange, angry man.**

The barely controlled violence she'd sensed in him frightened her. For a man who had been asleep only moments before, he was now completely alert, and watching her with an intensity that had the breath backing up in her throat. There was something dangerously primitive about this man.

"I was…" She swallowed and tried again, hoping her heart would settle. "I was just heading toward the kitchen. Would you like something to eat?"

For several more seconds he remained completely still, sensing her fear. The fact that he'd behaved instinctively didn't matter at the moment. Mere words couldn't explain his behavior. He could think of nothing that would make things right. Nor did he bother to try. How could he expect her to understand? What he was going through was his own private hell. He had no intention of sharing it with anyone else.

Her offer had him shaking his head. Right now the last thing he wanted was food. Or company. "No thanks. I'm not hungry."

"Well, then." She turned toward the door and prayed he wouldn't notice the way her legs were trembling. "I'll just fix something for myself. It's been a long day and I'm famished." She knew she was talking too fast. The words spilled out one on top of the other. But she wanted desperately to get away from this man. So desperately, she nearly ran in her haste to escape.

Over her shoulder she called, "If you get hungry later, help yourself to whatever you want."

She didn't wait for his response as she headed toward the kitchen. At the end of the hallway she stopped and turned around. A sigh of relief escaped her lips when she was satisfied that he hadn't followed her.

The last thing she wanted was to spend tonight in the company of a man who looked for all the world like a movie version of a professional hit man. A man who seemed to have more in common with the predators in the wild than with the gentlemen hunters who were the usual guests of the Snug Harbor Lodge.

"Oh, Grandpa Sully," she whispered as she pushed open the door to the kitchen and snapped on the overhead lights.

Her grandfather knew that she looked forward to the privacy of her off-season. Not only because it gave her precious time to repair, repaint and restore the equipment and the lodge, but also because it gave her precious time for herself. There were so many books to be read. Videos to be enjoyed. Music to be savored. Not to mention mountains to be climbed and trails to be hiked. Alone.

She smiled, just thinking about that word. To Alexandra Sullivan, the thought of spending time alone was the most cherished gift of all. Whether she was hiking alone, boating alone or sleeping alone, she never equated such things with being lonely. She treasured time to herself. And considered it essential to restoring her soul.

She shook her head in disbelief. Whatever had her grandfather been thinking, sending this strange, angry man into her life?

Chapter 2

Distracted, Grant prowled his room before turning to stare at the closed door. He could still feel the imprint of Alexandra Sullivan's body on his. What an unexpected shock it had been to his system. Without thinking he'd reacted to the threat of danger, only to find a very different sort than he'd imagined. In the space of a single heartbeat he'd been not only awakened, but fully aroused.

Alex Sullivan may be tall and slim, but the press of those soft curves had been a stunning reminder to him that she was all woman. And though his mind was still in a state of chaos, his body seemed to have no problem remembering how to react. That fact ought to please him. It had been some months now since he'd shown any interest in anyone or anything except the troubles that plagued him.

He walked to the window and peered out at the darkness, annoyed at the direction of his thoughts. The fact that she'd been able to enter his room and get close enough to touch him while he slept was proof that he was more exhausted than he realized. There had been a time when nobody could have accomplished such a feat. He'd always prided himself on having a sixth sense about such things. His friends had teased him about having eyes in the back of his head.

He listened to the sound of her soft footsteps as she passed his door and returned to her room. Heard the click of her door as she closed it. Minutes later he heard the soft strains of an orchestra and the pure clean voice of Italian tenor Andrea Bocelli. Not what he'd expected to hear in the middle of the New Hampshire wilderness. But then, nothing was what he'd expected so far. Least of all, Alex Sullivan. He couldn't get the thought of her out of his mind. Or the way she'd felt, pressed to the mattress beneath him. What would she taste like? The question tantalized him.

Like a caged animal he paced the length of the room before picking up a book from the pile on the desk. But when he sat down and tried to read, the sounds of the music from the next room kept distracting him. Bocelli's voice weeping over a lost love had him tossing aside the book with a hiss of disgust. To drown out the music he switched on the television. As he flipped through the channels, his eyes narrowed at the number of violent cop shows, and the scenes of death and destruction on the news. Finally, he found a cartoon and dropped onto the bed, determined to watch until it lulled him to sleep. But minutes later, as the cartoon dog and cat began tearing each other to shreds, he clicked off the set and sprang to his feet.

After more prowling, he decided he needed to escape these four walls. He emerged from the room and made his way along the darkened hallway until he came to the kitchen. Throwing on the light, he paused in the doorway, pulling himself back from his thoughts. Though this room appeared to be as rustic as the rest of the lodge, its decor was deceptive. On closer inspection he could see that it was as well equipped as any modern restaurant.

He let out a hiss of breath. "Not exactly what I'd expected to find in a simple hunting lodge."

"My family believes in efficiency and service to our guests."

The velvet voice behind him had him whirling.

"Sorry." She took a step back, seeing again that heat in his gaze. "I didn't mean to startle you. I was just coming out here for another cup of coffee. Can I get you something?"

''No. I...'' He paused to watch as she crossed the room. This was the second time she'd managed to sneak up on him. He was definitely losing his touch. ''Maybe I'll have one, too.''

''If you'd like to add whiskey to it, there's some in the bar pantry.'' She pointed. ''Help yourself.''

He opened the pantry and studied the array of bottles. ''This is pretty impressive.''

Alex gave a smile of satisfaction as she looked around. ''We have a walk-in cooler, a freezer stocked with the finest cuts of meat and seafood and a wine cellar that would rival any of the other hotels and inns in our chain.''

''How many hotels are there?'' Not that he cared. But he thought it wise to make idle conversation after that scene in his room. Something impersonal to keep him from thinking about the way she'd felt in his arms.

''At the moment, more than a dozen.''

Grant selected a bottle of Jack Daniels and closed the pantry door. ''All family-operated?''

''Not all.'' She laughed. ''There aren't enough Sullivans to go around. But we're working on it.''

He paused to study the bottles of wine behind the glass doors of the temperature-controlled wine cellar before turning to Alex, who was pouring two cups of coffee.

She'd brushed her hair long and loose and it flowed in soft waves past her shoulders. He'd thought at first it was brown, but now he could see that it was the color of honey. Warm, rich and lush. And her eyes weren't brown but rather a shade of amber.

She was wrapped in a bulky white robe with the shamrock green Sullivan crest on one pocket. A simple hotel robe, he realized. But on her it looked anything but simple. He found himself wondering what she wore underneath.

She looked at him over the rim of her cup. ''There's fresh chicken salad in the fridge if you're hungry.''

''This is enough.'' He splashed whiskey into his cup and tasted it before he began to prowl the room, studying the six-burner stove, the oversize ovens.

''Is it always this quiet around here?''

She nodded. ''Especially this time of year.''

She found herself fascinated by the way he studied everything, as though memorizing his surroundings. He had a cat-like way of moving that was unnerving. She would have sworn he'd already noted every door and window, as though expecting an army of invaders to burst through at any moment.

''Where are you from, Grant?''

''New York City.''

She chuckled. ''No wonder you're intrigued by the silence.''

"I haven't figured out whether I'm intrigued or annoyed by it."

She smiled. "Whenever I go up to New York, I'm nearly overwhelmed by all the sounds of the city. In fact, even on the top floor of a hotel, I swear I can hear the traffic far below."

She lifted the coffeemaker. "Want a little more before I unplug it?"

"Sure." He set his cup on the counter. "May as well…"

There was a sudden crash outside the door, followed by a thumping sound.

Grant reacted so quickly, Alex didn't even have time to utter a sound. In one violent sweep of his arm he shoved her behind him and reached instinctively for his pistol. When he realized that it was still in the drawer of his nightstand, he swore and reached for a kitchen knife before striding toward the back door.

"Grant, wait…"

He swung his gaze to Alex. She was stunned by the fierceness of his expression. It was a frightening thing to see. "Stay there." His voice had the authority of command.

"But I…" She started after him.

He closed a hand around her upper arm and shoved her back none too gently against a pantry door. "I said stay here. I want you safe until I see who's out there."

He turned away and flung open the door.

It occurred to Alex in that moment that Grant Malone wasn't just nervous or edgy. He was a man obsessed with danger. He anticipated it. Expected it. And faced it head-on. He wouldn't be a man to cross.

She waited until he stepped outside before throwing on the floodlights. Three raccoons looked up, blinking in the blinding light. One had been wriggling about in an overturned garbage can. A second was just knocking off the metal lid of another can. A third was rummaging through the remains of a plastic bag filled with potato skins and chicken bones.

"Go on." Alex flailed her arms. "Get out of here." As the three masked villains scurried away, she shook her head. "Those three little pests have become my nightly scourge. I never know where I'll find them. Eating the garbage. Trying to chew through the roof. Tunneling under my maintenance shed. Lem and I call them Larry, Moe and Curly."

Grant's arm dropped weakly at his side. He glanced at the knife, still clutched in his hand. Maybe it was the ridiculousness of the situation. Or maybe it was simply the surge of relief. Whatever the reason he began to laugh softly while shaking his head from side to side.

"Sorry. I guess it's going to take me awhile to forget I'm not back in the city."

"Yeah." Alex righted the trashcan and began scooping up the litter. When the back porch was cleared of debris, she turned and made her way inside.

As Grant followed, he realized that, though she'd managed a weak smile, she'd been watching him with that same look of concern she'd worn earlier, during that unfortunate scene in his bedroom.

He set the knife on the kitchen counter. "I'll say good-night now. Sorry about my overreaction to the raccoons."

She shrugged. "No harm done."

But there had been, he realized. Whatever relaxed mood they'd managed to create for a couple of minutes, it was now shattered. And it had all been his fault.

As he made his way to his bedroom, he cursed and called himself every kind of fool. A simple disturbance had sent him into a frenzy. He'd forgotten how to feel safe without a gun. He'd even forgotten how to walk into an unfamiliar room or carry on a simple conversation with a stranger without constantly looking over his shoulder. The violence of his world had chipped away at his humanity, until he'd forgotten how to live without calling up the violence within himself at every turn.

He was afraid the doctors were wrong. The man

he'd once been was gone. In his place was a loose
cannon that threatened to go off at any moment.

Alex sipped another cup of coffee and sat brooding in front of the fire. She wasn't mistaken about
the way Grant had behaved when she'd entered his
room. It had been the same in the kitchen. In both
instances there had been so much controlled violence in him, it frightened her.

Why was he here? She wished her grandfather
had told her more. She thought back over his
phone call. "I have a friend who has need of some
solitude. I immediately thought about the lodge,
and about the talent you have for handling
wounded critters. I know it's your off-season, darlin'. But I need to beg this favor."

How could she refuse her grandfather anything?
Her response had been immediate and uncondi-
tional. "What's his name, Grandpa Sully? And
when should I expect him?"

"That's my girl. I knew I could count on you,
darlin'. That's why I love you so."

The feeling was mutual. She adored her grandfather. If it weren't for him, she wouldn't be here
now, doing what she most loved in this life. Without this lodge, she might be running one of the
slick European hotels or spas that the Sullivan family owned and operated. And though she knew she
could do a good job, nothing would ever make her

as happy as this small corner of the world. It truly was her snug harbor. She couldn't imagine finding such joy anywhere else.

She sat a while longer, allowing her nerves to settle and her mood to lift. Whatever had happened to Grant Malone, it had left its mark on him. She would do what she did when treating one of the "critters" as her grandfather called the animals she nursed back to health. She'd give him time. Time to adjust to his surroundings. Time to learn to trust again. And in the meantime, she'd feed him, and give him plenty of privacy.

With a smile she banked the fire and headed down the hall.

As she passed Grant's room, she heard a soft moan. She paused, wishing she could comfort him. But she had no desire to risk his violent reaction again tonight. Instead she walked by and firmly closed the door to her room to block out any sound. She didn't want to peek inside Grant Malone's dreams. She had a sense that if she did, she would glimpse a nightmare.

As she undressed and crawled between the covers, she shivered, recalling the look in those eyes when he'd heard the sound of the garbage cans being overturned. There had been no fear in him. Nor was there the look of a wild-eyed fanatic. What she had seen was an icy, bloodless determination to face up to whatever was threatening his safety and hers, even at the cost of his life.

It was that calm, deadly acceptance of danger that frightened her the most. It was as though he had already anticipated its appearance, and was prepared to deal with it when it came.

What had happened to Grant Malone to make him this way? She shivered again and rolled to her side, determined to blot out all thought of the strange, angry man who had taken up residence in her lodge.

Alex moved the paintbrush in smooth, even strokes across the underside of the canoe. She wore stained sweats and a baseball cap to shade the bright autumn sunlight from her eyes.

Across from her, Lem was pouring paint from a larger bucket into a smaller one. The two had been working in companionable silence for more than three hours. It was what Alex loved most about the old man. When there was work to be done, he got to it, without any unnecessary small talk. There were days when they'd worked together from sunup to sundown without exchanging more than a dozen words.

He glanced up as the door of the lodge banged, and Grant stepped out onto the porch. "He just getting up?"

Alex shrugged. "Looks like it. I didn't see him

when I was fixing breakfast, so I figured he was still sleeping.''

She'd awakened through the night and heard footsteps along the hall. She assumed her guest couldn't sleep, and was prowling the kitchen or great room. And though she'd been curious, she'd forced herself to roll over and go back to sleep. What Grant Malone did in the long hours of the night was his own business. She was running a lodge, not a sleep-disturbance clinic.

''You get that sandwich in bed last night?''

She laughed. ''Yeah. By the time I got around to eating it, I was so hungry, I could have eaten a steak. Still on the hoof.''

He joined in her laughter. ''You grill one for your guest?''

She shook her head. ''He claimed he wasn't hungry.'' She didn't bother to mention the incident in Grant's bedroom. It still gave her an uneasy feeling to think about the strength in those hands, or the way she'd felt when she found herself pinned under him on the bed.

She wanted to tell herself it was purely fear. But a nagging little thought kept worrying the edge of her mind. Fear hadn't been the only thing she'd experienced in that moment. She'd been badly shaken by the feelings his touch had awakened in her. She experienced a keen excitement, as though she were standing on the very edge of a high, sheer

precipice. One step and she'd either fall straight
down or soar as high as an eagle.

"Maybe you'll get your wish and he won't get
his appetite back until he's headed home."

"Sure." She dragged herself back from her
thoughts, wondering what in the world was happening to her usually clear, sensible mind. "And
maybe by the end of the week I can have him
helping with the chores and doing the laundry."

That had them both chuckling.

They saw Grant step off the porch, before suddenly veering toward the woods.

"Looks like he's avoiding us." Lem picked up
a brush and started painting a second canoe.

"Maybe he just needs to be alone." She forced
herself to concentrate on the job.

"Was he still wearing that frown last night?"

"At first. But he finally seemed to be lightening
up." She paused, her paintbrush in midstroke. "I'd
just poured him a second cup of coffee when we
had our nightly visit from Larry, Moe and Curly."

"Ornery little critters. Remind me to empty the
garbage before I leave. No point in feeding guests
who won't pay."

She nodded absently, before describing Grant's
reaction to the sounds outside the door.

Lem grew thoughtful for a moment before saying, "Sounds like a mighty troubled man."

"Yeah."

He paused in his work and gave her a hard, steady look. "You feeling unsafe around him, Alex?"

She turned to meet his assessing gaze. "I don't have a sense that he'd do anything to me. Mainly because Grandpa Sully sent him up here. You know my grandfather would never do anything that would put me in harm's way." She shook her head slowly, choosing her words carefully. "But also because I just have this feeling about Grant Malone. He isn't so much a dangerous man as he is a tormented one. I think he's been through something..." She shrugged for emphasis. "...really painful. Something that has him seeing a threat at every shadow."

"Good thing it's not hunting season. No telling how he'd react if he found himself in these woods facing dozens of men with rifles."

Alex nodded, then bent to her work, lost in thought. It wouldn't surprise her to see Grant Malone face down a dozen men with rifles the same way he'd faced down Larry, Moe and Curly. With that same fierce expression and gung-ho attitude.

"Whatever emotions he's dealing with, I'm convinced that fear isn't one of them. But something's eating at his mind, Lem. And possibly at his heart and soul, as well."

He gave her another steady look. "You thinking

he's like one of those strays you're always taking in?''

"Of course not." She said it quickly, as much to convince herself as Lem. "He's not my business. I have enough to do around this place, without taking on the troubles of every guest who walks through the door."

"Uh-huh."

She brought her head up sharply. "What's that supposed to mean?"

"Nothing. I'm just thinking about that fox pup you once found half-drowned. Remember how he thanked you? As I recall, he bit clear to the bone."

She glanced down at the hand holding the paintbrush. She still carried the scar. And the lesson had been a good one, despite the pain involved. But the truth was, faced with the same scenario, and knowing her bittersweet reward, she'd do it again.

Her tender heart wasn't completely understood by her sisters, who referred to her as a sucker for any sad-eyed creature. Maybe that was so. But she simply couldn't turn away from any sort of suffering. Even when she knew she'd be better off to remain uninvolved.

Though she'd prefer to be a hardheaded realist, it simply wasn't possible. She wouldn't be able to sleep at night if she didn't at least make the effort to help a creature, any creature, in need.

As she returned to her painting, she couldn't get

Grant Malone out of her mind. She thought of the look in his eyes, and found herself thinking about all the wounded animals she'd seen up close. The look was the same. It was more than wounded. It was desperate. And though she wanted to remain uninvolved, she knew there was no way she could remain so for long.

She flexed her hand and felt the twinge of scar tissue along her thumb. When dealing with a man like Grant, the wound could be much more damaging than a mere bite. If she wasn't very careful, she could find herself drawn into his private hell.

Chapter 3

Grant tramped through the woods, feeling the crunch of leaves beneath his hiking boots. At first he walked aimlessly, so deep in thought he never even took notice of the things around him.

He'd spent a miserable night. He'd tried reading in bed. Had watched half of an old movie before giving it up and prowling the lodge. He'd made a fresh pot of coffee and had piled several logs on the fire. When, just before dawn, he finally returned to his room, he'd slept less than an hour before hearing Alex moving around. But he'd deliberately stayed in bed, avoiding her. He wasn't fit company. There were too many dark places in his mind. And he'd visited all of them in the past few hours, leaving him more on edge than ever. The last thing he needed was to inflict himself on others when he was in one of these moods.

When he came to a giant boulder, he paused, then stood back to study it, trying to figure out a way to climb it. It was, he decided, just his nature to have to solve every problem that presented itself.

It took half a dozen attempts, moving around it, hauling himself halfway up, then sliding back down, before he finally managed to scramble to the top. It didn't matter that his hands had been scraped raw, that he was breathless and sweating. It gave him an odd sense of satisfaction to be able to sit on his perch and see in all directions.

To his left was a thick stand of evergreens that formed a solid wall of forest. To his right the woods seemed less dense, but infinitely more colorful. Behind him the land rose gently, a series of hills covered with fiery foliage. In front of him loomed the lake. Off to one side of it was the lodge, looking every bit the millionaire's retreat it had once been, with its aged wood and clever use of stone, its windows gleaming in the afternoon sunlight. Though it had to be more than fifty years old, it was as bright and tidy as a new penny. It was obvious that the Snug Harbor Lodge was lovingly cared for.

There on the shore was the line of canoes, and

the old man and young woman looking just the
way they had yesterday when he'd arrived. Painting, occasionally pausing to refill their buckets or
to talk, then picking up their brushes to paint again.
They looked as much a part of this place as the
building and the land. He was, he realized, the only
thing that didn't fit.

He glanced beyond them. The surface of the lake
was as smooth as glass. For the first time Grant
noticed the way the trees were reflected in the water. It was a stunningly beautiful scene. He bent
one leg and wrapped his arms around his knee.
This was a view a man could drink in and never
tire of. The sun, the fiery autumn foliage, the
sounds of the woods around him were a soothing
balm to his battered soul.

He sat for the longest time, unmoving, as a long
line of geese drifted in a *V* across the sky and
slowly circled the lake. When they finally landed,
the water's surface was churned and turbulent before it calmed, and they began moving in lazy circles.

In his entire life Grant had never taken the time
to just sit and look and listen. It seemed at odds
with his nature to stand back and do nothing. To
have no plan. No schedule. No job to go to. No
one needing him. Depending on him. He frowned.
It ought to bother him. He was, after all, a man
who had always had a purpose. He liked being

needed. One of the shrinks had called him the perfect example of the alpha male. The man who needed no one but himself and his own wits to survive. And though he'd never given a thought to it, he liked the description and agreed with it.

He closed his eyes. It was so quiet here, he could hear the hum of an insect, the drone of a bee. The soft velvet peal of laughter carried on the breeze, followed by the deeper rumble of Lem's voice, and Grant found himself straining to catch a word or a phrase. It was nice to see two people who enjoyed each other's company so much.

Alex Sullivan had a wonderful voice and a relaxed, casual manner that made her easy to be around. What he liked best about her was that she didn't push. When he said he wanted to be alone, she took him at his word and gave him all the space he needed. She didn't feel she had to fill every silence with the sound of her own voice. In fact, she seemed as comfortable with silence as with sound.

No pretenses there, he thought. He'd bet everything he had that she was exactly what she appeared to be. A lovely young woman who seemed completely comfortable with herself and her choice of lifestyle.

He'd thought that about himself, not so very long ago. There had been a time when he'd loved his life, and held his career in the highest esteem.

He hadn't been able to see himself being or doing anything except who and what he was. Now he couldn't imagine going on with it. Each day he found himself questioning everything he'd ever believed in. The thought of facing another day on the job left him with a sense of dread. But without that job, there seemed an emptiness stretching out before him that nothing else could fill.

Give it time, Dr. Brady had told him. *Don't push yourself. You've been through a trauma. Even after the body heals, more time is needed for the mind and heart and soul to heal as well.*

Time. He stretched out on top of the flat rock and closed his eyes, feeling the heat of the sun against his lids. If all it took was time, he would have already mended. He lifted his hand and pressed it to his eyes. What he needed was something along the lines of a miracle.

Grant awoke feeling chilled. His eyes opened and he realized the sun had already made its arc across the sky and was setting behind a bank of low-hanging clouds.

How odd, he thought, that he could sleep here in the open, without feeling like a target. But then this boulder offered the perfect refuge. He was high enough to see in any direction. And too high to be seen by anyone passing by, unless they were specifically looking for him.

He slid down the side of the rock and began walking toward the lodge. As he drew closer he realized that Lem's truck was gone. He glanced toward the shore. The canoes were all wearing a fresh coat of paint.

Inside the lodge Alex was just emerging from her bedroom. Grant could tell, by the way her damp hair curled around her face, that she'd just come from the shower. She was wearing clean denims and a ribbed turtleneck. There was the faintest fragrance of something light and airy drifting around her.

"That was some walk in the woods. You must have put in ten miles or more."

He shook his head. "The truth is, I climbed up on a big flat boulder not far from here and fell asleep."

"I know exactly which boulder. I call it Tabletop. When I was little, I used to think it would make a perfect table for a giant."

"Yeah, it would." He tried not to stare at the way her sweater clung to those softly rounded curves. Up close he could see that her face was bare of makeup. Her skin was as flawless as porcelain.

"I'm thinking of making grilled cheese sandwiches and a big bowl of tomato soup. Hungry?"

He was tempted. But he wasn't ready for company yet. "No thanks. I'll help myself to something later."

"Okay." She turned away, and wondered at the little tug of disappointment. After all, she'd put in a long day of hard, physical work. All she really wanted was a quick meal and a chance to finish the book she'd started, and then a good night's sleep.

The last thing she needed, she told herself sternly, was another meal to fix. And maybe another scene like the one last night.

Later, when she carried her plate to her room, she saw no light on beneath Grant's door and found herself wondering if he was already asleep.

What a strange guest. She nudged her door closed and settled into bed to eat and read. Later, as she was falling asleep, she thought she heard a door open and close.

Maybe it was hunger that drove him to prowl during the night. Or maybe it was a desire to simply be alone. Whatever his reason, he was welcome to it. She had no intention of intruding on his privacy.

Exhausted, she slept.

When the cabin door slammed, Lem looked up from the boat engine he and Alex were working on. He saw Grant step outside in the afternoon sun.

"You two ever talk?"

"Barely." Which suited her just fine. She reached for the pliers and gave a twist before setting the fuel pump on the rag spread on the grass.

"He's been here for more'n a week now. What do you know about him?"

"Nothing. Except that he never smiles." She worked companionably beside Lem for the next several hours before setting the new pump in place.

She tightened the screws, and wiped her hands on a rag. "I think that does it for the boats. They'll be in good shape come spring."

Lem nodded. "You still want me to pick up a couple gallons of gas?"

"If you don't mind driving into town."

"Don't mind at all. I got a couple of errands to run for Marge anyhow." He glanced skyward, instead of glancing at his watch. "If I leave now, I can be home in time for supper."

"Okay. I'll see you tomorrow, Lem."

"Yep." He sauntered toward the truck.

Alex carried her tools to the shed, then made her way inside the lodge. As she filled the tub it occurred to her that having Grant Malone around wasn't so bad after all. They rarely spoke. He made no demands on her time.

She peeled off her filthy sweats and climbed into the scented water, sighing with the pure pleasure of it. She was already planning dinner. She would grill a steak and eat in her room. And get started on the new thriller she'd been dying to read.

Grant stood under the shower and let the hot spray beat on his chest. The hike today had been a challenge. Plenty of hills to climb, and rocks and fallen logs to maneuver across or around. Not quite as tough as a workout in the gym, but at least his muscles were protesting a bit. That was a good sign. He intended to push himself a little more each day, until he was back in peak shape.

He needed something more demanding. He thought about the chores that Alex and Lem shared. He wouldn't mind helping, but he didn't think he could be included in the work without also being invited to share their conversation. And he wasn't sure he was ready for that.

As he toweled himself dry and slipped into fresh denims, it occurred to him that he was hungry. This was the first time in weeks that he actually craved food. He finished dressing and headed down the hall.

In the kitchen Alex looked up when the door opened.

"I was just going to grill a steak. Want one?"

If he'd been caught unaware, he didn't show it. "Yeah. What can I do to help?"

She shrugged, too surprised for a moment to answer. Did this mean the mystery man actually ate food like humans?

"The salad fixings are in there." She pointed toward the refrigerator and smiled. "Do you know how to fix a salad?"

"I think I can manage." There was no answering smile.

"Okay. Salad bowls are up there." She nodded toward the cupboards.

He rolled up his sleeves, washed his hands, then began hauling out fresh greens. There were three kinds of lettuce. A dozen different vegetables, including sweet red and Vidalia onions, cucumbers, garden-ripened tomatoes. All washed and packaged in neatly-marked plastic containers.

He looked over at Alex, who had just retrieved two steaks from the cooler and was placing them on the grill. "I thought you said this was your off-season."

"It is."

"You mean you stocked all this for the two of us?"

"That's right." She shot him an impish grin. "Isn't it a comfort to know that you'll never go hungry?"

"I guess I figured here at the lodge you ate only what you were able to shoot or hook on a line."

"Are you kidding? If we lived by that rule, we'd starve. Even during the hunting and fishing season, when most of our guests try to outdo each other with the most exotic trophy or the biggest fish, it's not about dinner. Even though they're dedicated outdoorsmen, it's all about bragging rights. And these days, more of them hunt with a camera than with a rifle anyway." She gave him a sideways look. "I don't know if you've had a chance to taste photos of deer, but they don't make for a great dinner."

That brought a quick smile to his lips.

So the man could actually smile. That was a beginning.

She turned toward the bar. "Do you want wine? Or would you prefer beer?"

"I'll have a beer."

She opened two cans and poured them into frosted mugs, then handed him one.

"Thanks." He took a long pull, then watched as she returned to the grill to tend the steaks. It occurred to him that she had just about the best-looking backside he'd ever seen. He couldn't remember when he'd noticed a woman who looked better in a pair of faded denims.

She looked up. "Salads done yet?"

He turned away, reluctant to be caught staring. As an afterthought he added hearts-of-palm and beefsteak tomatoes to the salads. Then he studied the variety of dressings. "Looks like you bought

out the store. Do you have a favorite salad dressing?''

"Something simple. Maybe a little oil and bal-
samic vinegar."

"That works for me, too." Satisfied, he leaned
against the counter and drained his beer as Alex
set a tray of cheese rolls under the broiler. He bit
back a smile. Definitely a great view from where
he was standing.

She glanced over. "How do you want your
steak?"

"Medium-rare."

"Then it's just about ready." She placed the
rolls in a linen-lined basket and set it on a serving
tray before turning to him. "Would you rather eat
in the dining room, or in the great room in front
of the fire?"

"The great room, if you have no objections."

"None at all." She speared the two steaks and
placed them on a platter, then crossed to the
counter and set their salads on the tray.

Before she could lift it he surprised her by taking
the tray from her hands. She indicated a wheeled
serving cart loaded with china, napkins and silver.
"We can take everything on this."

He pushed the cart from the kitchen to the great
room. The fireplace was open on all four sides,
with comfortable sofas pulled close for warmth.

While Alex set two places on a low coffee table, Grant tossed another log on the fire.

"Funny." He settled himself beside her on the sofa. "When my grandfather talked about the Snug Harbor Lodge, I had a mental picture of this really rustic old cabin in the woods, with a couple of bunk beds and a scarred wooden table."

Alex broke open a roll. "Your grandfather stayed here?"

He nodded, and sipped his beer. "Every year for the past thirty years, I'd say."

She searched her mind, then shook her head. "I don't remember a Malone being here."

"He's not a Malone. He's my mother's father. Michael Finn."

"Mickey?" She gave him a long measuring look. "Mickey Finn is your grandfather?"

"Yeah."

"Why didn't you say so?"

He looked over. "I just did."

She started laughing. "I've known Mickey since I was just a kid. He and my grandfather, Grandpa Sully, have been friends since their college days."

"I know. That's all I heard about when I was little. How he and Sully bagged their first eight-point buck together. How Sully held the record for the biggest bass ever caught in this lake, until one of the other regulars here at the lodge beat him."

"Simon Taylor. Four years ago." Alex leaned

back, laughing. "And the two of them have been trying ever since to beat Simon's record."

Grant speared a bite of steak. "I've been hearing about the amazing Alex Sullivan for a couple of years now. How Alex led their party to the biggest herd of deer. Alex knew the perfect spot to toss a line and catch enough fish to feed an army. Alex once backpacked into the wilderness and returned a month later looking as relaxed as if it had been a walk in the park."

"Obviously Mickey exaggerated a bit."

He looked over. "I don't think so." He set down his fork and picked up his beer. "So why did you?"

"Why did I what?"

"Backpack into the wilderness and stay a month?"

She shrugged. "Just to see if I could survive alone."

"You weren't afraid?"

"Afraid?" She shook her head and leaned back. "These woods are home to me. When I was little, this place was my grandfather's refuge from the pressures of running a hotel. The first time I saw it, I was a nine-year-old tomboy, who fell head over heels in love. My sisters would never come here with Grandpa Sully after that first time. They preferred life in the city. But I think I always knew that this was where I wanted to live my life."

"You don't feel isolated in the winter, when the lodge is closed?"

She laughed. "Isolated? Look around. I have everything I need here."

He did look around. And he had to admit there was a feeling of comfort here. There was something solid and sturdy about this place. But there was no denying it was miles from its nearest neighbor.

He turned back to study her. "You don't feel lonely when everyone goes home for the winter?"

She shook her head and stared into the flames of the fire. "It's funny. Most of the men who come here have been coming to the lodge for years. Many are avid hunters, or just good friends of Grandpa Sully's. And now they're friends of mine, as well. While they're here, we're like one big family. I enjoy the teasing, the jokes, the good-natured competition among friends. But when everyone leaves, and I'm left on my own, I never feel lonely. There's so much to do. Not just the maintenance of the lodge and the grounds, but the books I've been waiting to read, the movies I've been waiting to see. Not to mention the trails I've been meaning to hike."

"So you take a busman's holiday, and hike just for the fun of it?"

"Yeah." Her eyes took on a dreamy look. "That's when it's the most fun. There's something so satisfying about knowing that I can sleep under the stars if I want to. And if I decide to take an extra day or two along the trail, nobody's plans will be spoiled. There's just me and nature.'' She stood. ''Want another beer?''

''Sure. Are you having one?''

She nodded and strolled away.

Grant found himself thinking about his own life. It couldn't be any more different. Alarm clocks and shifts and schedules. Mean streets. Tires screeching. Sirens. Throngs of people, all of them in a hurry. Some of them plotting death and destruction. But which of them? It was his job to figure that out. It was a life that had kept him living on the edge too long, until he'd cracked and lost a part of himself. And now he wasn't certain he'd ever be whole again.

''Here you go.'' Alex handed him a beer, and watched the way he struggled to pull himself back from whatever place he'd gone in his mind. ''I put on some coffee. It'll be ready in a few minutes.''

''Thanks.''

''Did your grandfather tell you how he and Grandpa Sully happened to become friends back in college?''

Grant shook his head.

Alex settled on the sofa and nudged off her shoes, extending her feet toward the warmth of the fire. ''They were both after the same girl. Colleen

O'Brien. They went to extravagant lengths to trip each other up, and nearly went broke buying expensive gifts to impress her. Then, after promising each of them that they could escort her to a New Year's Eve ball, Colleen ended up dumping them to go with a stodgy, pipe-smoking professor. Grandpa Sully said he and Mickey consoled each other over a bottle of gin, and became fast friends.''

''I wonder what ever happened to good old Colleen?'' Grant mused.

''According to Grandpa Sully she was all set to marry her professor until he met her mother and fell head over heels in love. The two ran off together and no one ever heard from them again.''

Grant smiled, and it occurred to Alex that he looked completely different when he was relaxed and smiling. ''Sounds like poetic justice.''

''That's exactly what Grandpa Sully and Mickey concluded.'' She stood and headed for the kitchen. ''How would you like your coffee?''

''Black.''

''I'll be right back.''

''Wait. I'll give you a hand.'' Grant drained his beer and began loading dishes onto the cart.

As he wheeled it toward the kitchen it occurred to him that he hadn't felt this relaxed in months. Maybe the experts were right. A change of pace.

A fresh face. A new environment. This was just what the doctor ordered.

In the kitchen Alex filled two cups with coffee and retrieved a bottle of brandy.

When she turned, Grant was already loading dishes into the dishwasher. "Hey, that's supposed to be my job. You're the guest here."

"It's your off-season. Remember?" He continued working until the cart was empty. "Besides, all you seem to do is work. Every time I look up, I see you and Lem finishing another chore."

"I didn't think you noticed."

His voice roughened slightly. "Yeah, I noticed." And he was noticing a whole lot more. The way a strand of her hair had drifted over her eye. The way her lips curved in a most appealing smile. And the way she smelled up close. As fresh and clean as a meadow in springtime.

She didn't know why, but his words, and the way he spoke them, caused a tiny flutter in the pit of her stomach. And the way he was watching her had her heart stuttering.

She handed him a cup. Their fingers brushed, and she felt the hair at the back of her neck begin to prickle. Some of the coffee sloshed over the rim of her cup and he reached out to grab it. That only made things worse. She drew back quickly, but his hand was there, steadying hers, taking the cup from her hand before she could burn herself.

"Thanks." She gave a shaky laugh. What in the world was wrong with her?

He lay a hand over hers and she felt a sudden wave of heat. "You okay?"

She nodded. "Yeah. I'm fine."

Grant kept his hand where it was, his eyes hot and steady on hers as he leaned close. Close enough that their mouths were almost touching.

In that instant Alex knew he was going to kiss her. And though she ought to be afraid, she felt strangely exhilarated as she waited for his lips to brush hers.

It was the merest touch of mouths. As soft, as tentative as a snowflake. But the moment their lips met, everything changed.

His hands closed over the tops of her arms, dragging her close. His mouth was no longer gentle but rough, almost savage as he kissed her with a hunger, a thoroughness that had her gasping.

All she could do was hang on as his mouth plundered hers. Their lips mated, and took from each other until they were both trembling with need.

In that instant she could feel her blood heating and her bones slowly melting as he took the kiss deeper. But never once did it occur to her to push away. She merely clung, returning his kiss with a passion that caught them both by surprise.

This was what he'd wanted. From the time he'd walked into the kitchen tonight, he'd thought about nothing but this. The way she would taste. As clean and fresh as a mountain stream. And the way she would feel in his arms. Soft and pliant, that lean body bending like a willow.

There was danger here he knew. The alarm bells were already sounding in his mind. His feelings were still too raw. And the beast inside him too savage to trust. Unless he ended this now, he might easily cross a line.

Still, he allowed himself one more taste as he dug his fingers into the tangles of her hair and drew her head back. One more taste of heaven before he returned to his own private hell.

He lifted his head.

It ended as quickly as it began. One minute he was devouring her; the next he had abruptly released her.

With stilted movements he stepped back. ''I'd say you're more than fine, Alex Sullivan.''

He picked up his coffee and turned toward the door. ''I think I'll take this to my room. I have…some reading to do.''

Without a word she watched as he strode away.

When he was gone she could do nothing more than stare at the closed door. How had that happened? When had a simple touch turned into a heart-stopping kiss?

She took a deep breath and prayed her pulse rate would soon return to its natural rhythm. When she could trust her trembling hands she picked up her cup and took a sip, then set it aside with a clatter.

Why in the world was she standing here feeling like she'd just been kissed for the first time in her life?

There had been plenty of men and plenty of kisses. But at the moment, she couldn't recall a single experience. Except this one. There had been such hunger in it. Such need. And for some strange reason she couldn't quite fathom, it had spoken to a similar hunger in her.

Dangerous ground, she cautioned herself. She was allowing herself to get too close to the wounded animal. And from the way he'd kissed her, there was definitely more animal in Grant Malone that she'd first expected.

Now if she could just keep in mind how a wounded animal reacted to anyone foolish enough to try to help.

Chapter 4

"What's this?" Lem was just pounding the last nail into the roof of the shed when he heard the lodge door slam and caught sight of Grant standing on the porch. "Looks like we made too much noise. Woke our night owl."

Alex looked over and felt the little thrill that inched along her spine. She'd spent a long night recalling that heart-shattering kiss.

Keeping her tone light she said, "He actually ate dinner last night, and went to bed at a sensible hour. At least I think he did. I didn't hear any footsteps during the night."

"That's comforting. Now you know he's probably not one of those vampires."

They both laughed.

Alex lowered her voice. "He surprised me. We exchanged a few stories about our grandfathers." She looked over at Lem. "His grandfather is Mickey Finn."

"You don't say?" The old man paused, hooked his hammer in his tool belt. "I've always liked Mickey. Tells great stories about his misspent youth."

Alex grinned. "I've heard a few. I still haven't figured out if they're true or a product of an over-active imagination."

"I figure he adds a bit of color to them. That's what makes them so much fun to hear." At the crunch of leaves, Lem lowered his voice. "Don't look now, but your guest is heading this way. Looks like he might even be planning to speak."

Grant paused beneath their ladders and tipped his head back to call, "Could you use some help?"

Lem stared down. "You ever use a hammer?"

"Now and again."

The old man nodded his approval. "There's another ladder in the shed. Tools on the bench. Nails in a bucket by the door. You can use Alex's tool belt. She won't be needing it."

Alex glanced at the old man. "And what am I supposed to do while you two handle this?"

"Seems to me you were worrying about getting tarps over all those canoes now that they're dry."

She grinned. "That's right."

"No time like the present."

She nodded and climbed down the ladder. As she handed Grant her tool belt she felt the heat on her cheeks. "You sure you want to tackle this?"

His eyes were steady on hers, and she felt certain he could see her discomfort. Was sure that he was recalling their kiss. But it was clear that he wasn't suffering any pangs of conscience. "I'm sure."

"Okay." She turned away abruptly and grabbed hold of a folded tarp before heading toward the line of canoes along the shore.

Grant stared after her until he realized Lem was watching. Then he turned away and climbed the ladder.

Grant stepped from the shower and toweled himself dry before pulling on clean denims and a flannel shirt. It had been a satisfying day. He'd been able to work beside Lem without having to talk about himself. But though the old man could be abrupt, he'd proven to have a sense of humor. Especially when Grant had asked him whether or not anybody looked out for Alex when the lodge was closed for the winter.

"You thinking Alex needs someone to look out for her?"

"She's a woman alone in the wilderness."

"Son, she's more at home in these woods than

the deer. And better able to take care of herself. She's been hiking in these mountains since she was just a kitten. And if there was ever a contest between Alex and Mother Nature, I'd put my money on Alex.''

"Have you known her for a lifetime?''

"Just about.'' The old man leaned on his ladder and glanced at the young woman on the shore of the lake. "I remember the first time she came here with her two sisters. All pretty little things. But the other two stayed pretty close to the lodge. Not Alex. Every waking minute she was off with her grandfather. Tugging on the oars of a boat. Splashing in the lake. Climbing trees. On their first hike, the other two sat down and refused to go another mile. Alex and her grandfather went on ahead, and left her two sisters with the lodge manager, Buck Thornton. Hours later, when they returned to the lodge, Alex had scratches and cuts all over her arms and legs. And she was as happy as if she'd just been given the keys to a toy store. I swear, that one had just found heaven. And it's been that way for her ever since. Whenever she has to leave, you'd think she was going to her own funeral. The minute she returns, she's as happy as a duck in a pond.''

As Grant made his way to the kitchen, he smiled. Maybe the old man was right. From what he'd seen so far, Alex was more than capable of taking care of herself in this wilderness.

When he opened the door, Alex looked up. "I thought I'd grill chicken and peppers. Should I grill enough for two?"

"Yeah. I think I've worked up quite an appetite." And not just for food, he realized. "Want some help?"

"Would you like to fix the salads again?"

"Instead of salads, why don't I make my famous nachos and hot salsa."

She shrugged. "I'm not sure I have any salsa."

"I'll make some." He began chopping tomatoes, onions and peppers.

Several times while he worked Alex glanced over. It occurred to her that he seemed more relaxed tonight. Without that perpetual frown, he was really handsome. His dark hair was cut military-short, giving him the look of a tough drill sergeant. But his eyes showed a light of amusement that hadn't been there before, softening the look somewhat.

He'd rolled the sleeves of his flannel shirt. It stretched tautly across shoulders that were corded with muscles. She thought again about the strength in those arms when he'd hauled her across his bed, and later when he'd pushed her roughly aside, thinking they were being threatened by the noise on the back porch.

But it wasn't a weapon she'd been thinking about last night when he'd kissed her. It had been a hard, muscled body pressed to hers. And her thoughts were hardly about warfare…

The thought made her suddenly too warm.

"Here." He paused alongside her, catching her by surprise.

She turned to find him holding out a glass.

"I thought I'd make something cold to enjoy with my hot salsa." He handed her a drink and as their fingers brushed, she felt another flash of heat. "A Margarita. Enjoy."

She brought it to her lips, tasted, then smiled. "Mmm. That's delicious. Thanks."

"How's the chicken coming along?" He remained beside her and she could almost feel the heat from his body.

"Almost done. Just a few more minutes."

"Good. Leave it and enjoy some of my nachos." He led the way to the kitchen counter, where he'd set out a platter.

Alex tasted, then sighed. "This is really good."

"I'm glad you like it." He indicated a bar stool beside the counter. "Here. Sit awhile and relax. You've put in a full day."

"The chicken…"

"I'll turn the chicken." He sauntered away, then returned to nibble more chips and salsa.

"They're really good." It occurred to Alex that

the heat was back. It hadn't been her imagination. Whenever he got close to her, she felt a rush of warmth that had nothing to do with the grill.

"I'm glad you're enjoying them." He leaned over her to help himself to another nacho. As he did he breathed her in. She smelled of lavender. He imagined that the scent would be even stronger at the base of her throat.

His own throat went dry at the thought, and he knew that sooner or later he was going to have to check it out for himself. The thought raised his temperature another notch. "I'd better put that chicken on a platter. Where did you want to eat tonight?"

She shrugged. "Your call."

"Good. I choose the great room again. I'm in the mood for a hot fire."

"To go with the hot food," she said with a laugh.

"Yeah." And, he thought, hot sex wouldn't be bad either. The idea had him sweating.

He set the grilled chicken and vegetables on a platter, then added the chips and salsa and the pitcher of Margaritas. "Have I forgotten anything?"

She slid from the stool to follow him. "With all this heat, we may need a pitcher of ice water."

"If we do, I'll come back for it." He pushed

the cart through the doorway and stopped beside the sofa.

While Alex arranged their plates and silverware, he tossed another log on the fire. Then they settled side by side on the sofa.

Grant lifted his glass to hers. "Here's to a job well done."

"I want to thank you, Grant. You and Lem got a lot done today." She brought her glass to her lips and drank, then sighed. "This is so nice. I wasn't expecting something as interesting as salsa and Margaritas. But they really hit the spot."

"Just happy to oblige, ma'am." He dipped a chip in salsa and held it out to her.

She had no choice but to accept. But when she reached out for it, he surprised her by guiding it to her mouth. As she opened her mouth she saw his eyes narrow and she absorbed a shaft of heat that went straight through her heart.

He was doing it again. With a single look he had her hot and cold and completely ill at ease.

Flustered she turned away and busied herself spooning chicken and vegetables onto her plate. When she looked up, he was still watching her in that quiet, intense way that caused her heart to miss several beats.

She picked up her glass and sipped, hoping for time to compose herself.

"So." She set aside her drink and began to eat.

"What do you think of the scenery here at the lodge?"

"Amazing." He stared pointedly at her. "The more I see, the more I like." He saw the color rise to her cheeks and knew that she'd caught his meaning. It almost made him smile.

He helped himself to dinner. "Is it my imagination, or does food taste better here?"

"It could be because this is the first meal you've had all day."

"Hmm. That's a distinct possibility."

She took another sip of her drink. "I've always found my appetite sharper here in the woods. Whenever I take myself off to civilization, I'm not nearly as hungry as when I'm home."

"Where do you go when you're not here?" He leaned back, willing himself to relax. It wasn't as difficult as he'd imagined. There was something about Alex, and the fire and this room that put him at ease.

"Well, there are my two sisters who live here in New Hampshire. Lizbeth lives in the town of Stafford, and runs a cozy little bed and breakfast. My sister Celeste runs the Old Liberty Tavern, a historic inn in Liberty, New Hampshire. I try to visit them whenever I'm not too busy here at the lodge. And my parents currently run Fielding Manor outside London. I had a wonderful visit with them last year. And, of course, Grandpa Sully, whose pride and joy is The Villa Maria in Lake Como. That's where I trained, and where I often return, just so I can spend time with him."

He was watching her eyes while she spoke. They simply sparkled whenever she mentioned one of her family. Fascinating, he thought, and wanted to see if it would happen again. "Any more family? Or is that all of them?"

"Oh! Don't get me started." She laughed, that warm, liquid velvet sound that had a way of wrapping itself around his heart. And tugging. "There are Aunt Miriam and Uncle Phil in Venice. Their son, Rob, who just took over our ski lodge in Aspen. Uncle Hugh and his daughter, Fiona, who've been overseeing Castle Dunniefey in Dublin. My cousin Mark and his wife, Leah, in Vermont, and his brother, Adam, who just left for Paris. All of them in the hotel business."

He lifted the pitcher, but before he could top off her glass she shook her head. "No more, thanks. I'm feeling pleasantly relaxed as it is. Anymore will just put me to sleep."

She watched as he added the last of the salsa to his chicken. "You really do like it hot, don't you?"

"Just seems a shame to waste it." He polished off his meal, and ate the last of the nacho chips as well. But even he couldn't finish the rest of the Margarita in the pitcher.

As Alex began to gather up the dishes, Grant brought the wheeled cart close and helped her load it. Then he pushed it to the kitchen while she trailed behind.

She indicated the coffeemaker. "Ready for some?"

"Sure. If you're making it."

Within minutes the kitchen was filled with the wonderful aroma of freshly ground coffee beans.

Alex set two cups on a silver tray, along with cinnamon sticks and a small tin of chocolate. When the coffee was ready she poured. As she did, a lock of her hair fell forward over one eye. When she looked up Grant was standing beside her. Before accepting the cup from her hand, he reached up to tuck her hair behind her ear. It was an oddly intimate gesture that had her heart doing a series of somersaults.

Grant looked down into those eyes, wide with surprise. He hadn't intended to touch her. It had been a purely spontaneous gesture. But now that he had, he couldn't seem to stop himself from pressing closer. "I don't know what smells better. You or that coffee."

"Careful." She backed up and felt the edge of the counter dig into her back. "You wouldn't want me to spill this."

He glanced down at her hand and was pleased

to note that it was trembling. Could it be that she was as affected by the touch as he had been?

"No. We wouldn't want that." He'd fully intended to walk away, but he found he couldn't. He simply had to push the boundaries a little more.

Her smile faded when he took the cup from her hand and set it on the counter, then smoothly moved in closer, invading her space. "There. That's better."

Better, maybe. But certainly not safer. For Alex there was nowhere to go. And nothing to do but try to pretend that this didn't bother her. Not an easy thing to do when her heart was thundering in her chest like a runaway train.

He brought his face so close to her throat she could feel the whisper of his breath on her flesh. "What's that perfume you're wearing?"

For the space of a heartbeat her mind went totally blank. All she could think of was the way her body strained toward his. "Em…" She swallowed. Tried again. "Embrace."

His gaze slid up to hers. Held. She saw his eyes heat. This was a dangerous game they were playing. But neither of them seemed able to call a halt to it. "It suits you."

It seemed, to Alex, that everything was happening in slow motion. The way he lifted his hands to her shoulders, to run them slowly down her arms. The way he breathed her in as he drew her close and nuzzled her cheek, her jaw, the corner of her mouth.

She waited, afraid to breathe, her heart afraid to beat, as he ever-so-slowly fitted his mouth to hers.

She was wonderful to watch. With his eyes steady on hers, he kissed her, noting the way her eyes widened for a moment before the lashes fluttered, then closed as she lost herself in the kiss. There was the slightest flush on her cheeks that betrayed the excitement she tried to hide.

Her hands lifted to his chest. Though she was unaware of it, her fingers closed around the front of his shirt and drew him even closer. Her breath came out in a sigh of pleasure.

He'd thought this time he could keep the kiss light. But it was impossible. The moment their lips met, he experienced an explosion of feelings that had him dragging her roughly into his arms and kissing her until they were both breathless. She tasted like sin. Hot and sweet and oh-so-tempting. And the more he tasted, the more he wanted. What he wanted most, he realized, was everything. All she had to give and more.

There was no tenderness in the kiss now, only a rough sort of savageness that excited her even while it frightened her. His mouth moved over hers, no longer merely taking, but demanding. And the hands at her back were almost bruising in their intensity as they moved over her body, touching at will.

She couldn't seem to engage her mind. She was helpless to stop him. With each touch, each taste, she found herself responding with a passion that shocked her. No man had ever taken her on such a wild, roller-coaster ride. And with nothing more than a kiss.

Dear heaven, what would it be like to give in to the needs driving her, and make love with such a man?

She wondered if she'd spoken the thought aloud. In that same instant, as though wondering himself, he lifted his head and lowered his hands to his sides. He took an experimental step back, as if to see if he could do so without stumbling.

His lips curved in a smile. As though, she thought, he was feeling extremely pleased with what he'd discovered.

"I think it would be a wise thing if I said good-night now, Alex."

"Yes." Her voice seemed to come from far away, and sounded strange in her own ears. "I'm feeling a bit tired myself."

"Yeah. I can see that." His smile grew as, with slow, easy movements, he took another step back and reached for the cup. Then he turned away.

Alex stood where she was, telling herself to breathe in and out. As her heartbeat returned to normal, she was grateful for the support of the kitchen counter behind her. Without it she was fairly certain she would have simply slid bonelessly to the floor.

Alex peeled off her clothes and slipped into flannel pajamas. Ordinarily she would simply climb into bed, turn out the light, roll to her side and be asleep within minutes. It was her nightly routine. After all, she'd been engaged in hard, physical work since early morning. It was natural to assume that her body craved rest. But tonight wasn't like most nights. She knew, before even getting into bed, that sleep would be a long time coming.

And all because of Grant Malone. Damn him for firing her blood and jumbling all her emotions. She couldn't remember the last time she'd felt so disconnected.

She first programmed her disk player with several soothing albums, hoping they could put her in the proper mood.

Proper mood. She winced. She'd been in the proper mood, all right. It would have taken no effort at all on his part to coax her into his bed. The minute he'd kissed her, she'd lost all her common sense.

What was it about this moody, troubled man that had her reacting like a girl with her first crush? Even now, just thinking about the look in his eyes had her heart racing, her palms sweating. What in the world was happening to her? She wanted, right this minute, to feel his kiss again. Wanted to feel again the tightly controlled strength in those arms. To have that muscled body pressed to hers.

He would be an exciting lover.

She sat on the edge of the bed and turned out the light, then dragged both hands through her tousled hair.

Enough of this, she cautioned herself. She was apt to be alone with this man for several weeks or more. The last thing she needed was to start entertaining any ideas about romancing a guest. Especially one as troubled and tense as Grant Malone.

What she needed, she decided, was something a bit more physically demanding for the next few days.

First thing in the morning, she and Lem would double their workload. There were windows to caulk and seal. Steps to be repaired on the back porch. A section of the roof that had begun leaking. Those chores ought to be enough to keep her from thinking about anything as foolish as falling into Grant's arms.

She lay down and snuggled under the blankets. From her stereo came the voice of Tony Bennett crooning about leaving his heart in San Francisco.

She had no intention of leaving hers anywhere. It was just fine where it was. Safe. Intact. Untouched.

She closed her eyes. Rolled to her side. And waited for sleep.

Chapter 5

Grant leaned a hip against the windowsill in the great room and stared out into the darkness. He was barefoot and shirtless. His jeans, unsnapped, rode low on his hips. He'd undressed, and had even climbed into bed, before giving up on the idea. Finally, he'd rolled out of bed, pulled on his jeans and stormed out of his room.

Although it was late, he knew it was useless to try to sleep. He was far too restless. He'd like to think it was because of all the things that had driven him to seek refuge here in the first place. But there was no denying the truth. It was because of the woman who lay asleep just down the hall.

He'd never felt anything quite like the quick sizzle of need that he'd experienced tonight. With little more than the touch of her lips, he'd been completely aroused. It had taken all his willpower to step back. But even now, just thinking about it, he wished it had been otherwise. He'd seen something in her eyes. Something as hot, as dangerous, as the feelings he was experiencing. Unless he'd misread her, she'd been as caught up in the moment as he.

He pressed his forehead to the cold windowpane, hoping to cool the fever that raged. Bad timing, he reminded himself. His system was already overloaded. The last thing he needed in his complicated life was one more complication. And Alex Sullivan was definitely that. A complication he simply couldn't afford right now.

Across the room, the fire had burned itself out, until all that remained were gleaming coals. Grant turned, intent on tossing another log on the grate.

Before he could move, he heard a sound and looked up to see a figure flitting through the shadows. He froze. In almost the same instant, he realized the figure was Alex.

He watched as she moved unerringly through the dark to the kitchen. Minutes later he heard the refrigerator door open and close; saw the light spill into the room, then fade. Before he could slip away to his room she returned.

He remained in the shadows, hoping she would leave and go back to her bedroom without noticing him. Instead she paused in front of the fireplace, to stare down into the gleaming coals.

She was barefoot, her hair streaming long and loose down her back, and wearing simple, men's-tailored pajamas. Grant thought he'd never seen anyone look more appealing. He studied her profile. She looked pensive. As disturbed as he'd been this past hour.

She sighed. Deep in thought she lifted a glass of milk to her lips and drank, before turning away.

Out of the corner of her eye she caught a slight movement. She let out a shriek and the glass tipped, sloshing milk over the rim before she managed to right it, grasping it in both hands.

"Grant." His name came out in a whoosh of air.

"Sorry." He stepped closer. "I didn't mean to startle you."

"I thought you were in bed. I saw a light under your door."

"I tried to sleep." He shrugged. "When I couldn't, I just figured I'd come out here for a while."

Now that her eyes had adjusted to the dim light, she could see that he was barely dressed. The sight of that half-naked body was doing strange things to her.

She lowered her gaze. "I...couldn't sleep either. I thought maybe some milk would help." She felt foolish staring at the glass in her hands. But she didn't know where else to look.

"It's dripping." He pried the glass away and set it on a table. Then he reached into his back pocket and withdrew a clean handkerchief, which he used to dry her fingers.

At once the heat was back. Searing her flesh. Firing her blood. The mere touch of him had her system going haywire. "Thanks. You don't…have to do…" She looked up. His eyes were in shadow, but she could tell he was staring at her the same way he'd stared earlier tonight.

She needed to escape. Quickly. Before she did something foolish. She started to turn away. "I'd better…" Her words were cut off abruptly when he closed his hands over her upper arms.

"Alex." His voice was deeper than usual. Rough with an emotion that might have been impatience or frustration. "You don't really think we can turn away from this a second time."

"We have to." She touched a hand to his chest to push him away, then drew it back abruptly.

"No, we don't." In the same instant he drew her firmly against him and lowered his head, until his mouth hovered just above hers. His eyes were as heated as his touch. "This time we have to finish it."

Without giving her time to disagree, his lips covered hers. There was nothing soft or tentative about the kiss. A kiss so hungry she felt herself drawn completely into it. His mouth moved over hers, taking, demanding, while his hands moved up her arms, across her shoulders, then slowly down her spine, pressing her to the length of him.

Alex felt her head swim as he changed the angle and took the kiss deeper. She felt the need rise up until a moan sounded low in her throat. A moan that sounded more animal than human.

It would be so easy to take what he offered. To allow herself to be taken. But it wouldn't be right. Not for either of them. This was madness. But where had it come from?

She jerked back and for the first time in her life was nearly overcome with fear. A fear that had her by the throat and was choking her. She wanted to run. To hide from whatever it was in this man that had turned her knees to jelly and her mind to mush.

"You can't… I won't…" Her face had gone pale. Her eyes wide.

He recognized the fear in them. But there was something else as well. The stirrings of something much deeper. And infinitely more dangerous for both of them. Passion. Hunger. He'd tasted it on her lips. Could read it in her eyes. Emotions that mirrored his own.

"I have to…" She started to pull away but he was quicker.

In one smooth motion he dragged her close and

savaged her mouth. His hands were equally rough, almost bruising in their intensity as they moved over her.

She could feel the barely controlled tension in him. It only served to excite her more. Her head swam. Her blood ran hot, surging through her veins, leaving her too weak to do more than hold on as he took her on a heart-stopping, head-spinning ride.

This was insane. She'd never felt such heat from a single kiss. Nor such need. It vibrated through her, catching her by surprise. She wanted him. Wanted this. Wanted more of the heat and the passion and the need.

When her hands circled his neck and fisted in his hair, he forgot everything except the woman in his arms. His grasp tightened. The kiss deepened. His hands moved down her back, loving the softness of flannel. At the moment it seemed more erotic to him than silk. When his fingers moved beneath the fabric to find her flesh, he felt a wave of desire that staggered him. He was desperate to touch her everywhere.

It was her little cry that brought him back to earth with a jolt. Until then he hadn't realized he'd actually lifted her off her feet. It shamed him to realize he'd forgotten his own strength. He'd practically crushed her in his arms.

He set her down almost roughly, before taking a step back, drawing air into his starving lungs.

Alex stood breathing deeply, waiting for her heart to settle. She could see him doing the same. And watching her in that strange, intense way that always managed to unnerve her.

Before she could find her voice he turned away. Without looking at her he said, "If you're smart you'll run back to your room as fast as you can and lock the door."

He turned then, and she caught a glimpse of something dark and dangerous in his eyes. "Now, Alex. Before we do something we'll both regret."

Without another word she turned and fled down the hall.

He waited until he heard her door close. Then he pressed both hands to the window and stared morosely out into the darkness. And willed himself to stay where he was rather than give in to the almost overpowering temptation to storm her room and take what he wanted.

In the days that followed, Alex threw herself into a frenzy of work. If Lem noticed that she was a bit tense, he wrote it off as prewinter jitters.

"Happens every autumn," he muttered to Grant as the two men passed each other on the front porch.

"What does?"

"That." He nodded toward Alex, who was busy sawing a dangling limb from a nearby tree. "Has to have everything ready before the first snowfall. See those weak tree branches? Could be dangerous if they got too heavy with snow. They're close enough to the roof to cause plenty of damage."

"Yeah." Grant paused to admire the way she looked on the ladder, her cheeks as red as apples, her hair fluttering on the breeze. "I suppose once the snows fall, she'll be pretty much on her own here at the lodge."

The older man nodded. "Marge, that's the wife," he explained with a fleeting smile, then started over. "Marge and I keep in contact with her by phone, but sometimes I can't get up here. Just digging out of my own driveway can take a day or more. And sometimes the road from my place to the lodge is closed. Not that we worry about Alex. No matter how bad the storms or deep the snow, she's always the same. Busy and cheerful."

Lem noticed the backpack. "Where're you off to?"

Grant tore his gaze from the woman on the ladder to look at the old man. He shrugged. "Wherever the trail takes me."

In order to put some distance between himself and Alex, he'd begun leaving early in the morning, and not returning until early evening, when the sun was already far below the tree line. For the past couple of mornings he and Lem had taken a moment to pause and exchange a few words before going their separate ways.

As Grant took his leave, Lem put away his tools and stepped out of the shed. Alex was just setting a ladder against the side of the lodge.

"Starting early this morning, aren't you?"

She turned. "Figured I'd get at it while the weather held."

"Saw your guest."

She'd seen him as well. And had been forced to endure a quick jolt to her heart before getting back to her work. She kicked mud off her boots and started to climb. "Did he say where he was going?"

"Just off by himself." The old man held the ladder steady. "Don't the two of you ever talk?"

She shrugged and reached for the caulking gun. "Not unless we have to."

"Does that mean he's still brooding?"

She glanced down. "He seems to have a lot on his mind."

"How about over supper? Don't the two of you discuss what you did all day?"

"Sometimes." She bent to her work, hoping Lem would let it go. The truth was, she and Grant had spent the past couple of evenings dancing gingerly around each other, trying not to think about the feelings they'd unearthed.

Just thinking about it had Alex sweating. She struggled to shut out the image of Grant from her mind. But it was impossible. The harder she tried, the more indelible seemed the sight of him, like some fierce, half-naked savage, drawing her in with no more than a look.

In truth, that's what frightened her the most. Not the seething tension she'd felt in him, or the raw passion, but the ease with which she'd given herself up to it. She knew nothing about this man, but had practically thrown herself into his arms. With no more than a simple kiss, he'd lit a fuse in her that was still setting off explosions.

A simple kiss. She closed her eyes against the thought of it. There was nothing simple about the way he'd kissed her. In her entire life, she'd never experienced anything quite like it. And she couldn't even figure out why it had been so shattering. She'd been drawn into something so overpowering, she'd been helpless to slow it down, or even try to put on the brakes.

There just seemed to be something in her that had responded to the very brooding, very mysterious Grant Malone.

This could prove to be a delicate situation. They were, after all, sharing a pretty confining space.

And she still had no idea how long he intended to stay.

"I see you didn't do this one yet."

Alex pulled herself back from her thoughts to glance over at Lem. He was standing on a ladder at the far end of the lodge.

"No. I thought I'd start on this end."

"Okay. I'll work my way over. We'll meet somewhere in the middle."

"Fine." She paused a moment. Maybe that was what she and Grant ought to strive for. Meeting somewhere in the middle. They couldn't keep avoiding each other. The lodge was too small. There was nowhere to hide. Besides, until that kiss, she'd enjoyed their dinners together. She wanted to get back to that easy feeling. She wanted to laugh with him. Exchange stories about their grandfathers.

Devour him in one single bite.

She winced, then returned her attention to the job at hand. Tonight she would stop hiding in her room. She'd make dinner and invite him to join her in the great room. She'd keep the conversation simple, the mood light. And maybe, just maybe, they could get back on track.

Grant climbed to the very top of the wooded hill and paused to catch his breath before turning to enjoy the view. He'd hiked to the far side of the lake, and was standing on the highest point. From here he could see the lodge, looking like a sparkling jewel in the autumn sunshine.

He'd begun to look forward to these treks. Not only did they test his endurance, but they forced him to step outside himself. To stand back from his problems and simply enjoy the beauty of nature.

In the bustling city there had been no time to mark the changing seasons. In his line of work, one season was pretty much like another. And all of them brought their own particular set of problems.

Here, so far from civilization, he'd become aware of so many things he'd never noticed before. He could actually see the days growing shorter, as morning arrived a little later and dusk settled a little sooner. In the city, with all its neon, it had never been so noticeable. But out here, everything about nature was so clear. The way little clouds of mist formed over the lake as the morning sun began to rise, warming the water. The way the air seemed perfumed with so many different scents. Pungent earth and sweet, clean evergreen and spicy apple.

He slipped off the backpack and sat in the grass. And found his thoughts returning to Alex. He loved the way she smelled. Light, delicate. Like a field of wildflowers. He could still taste her. As fresh and clean as a woodland stream in winter. And the way she'd felt in his arms.

One touch and he'd been on fire.

What was he going to do about this? If he couldn't find a way to ease the tension between them, he'd have to go. Not that he wanted to. This place had actually been a last resort. He'd already tried the shrinks and the pills. Meditation. Yoga. Working out until his body had protested and refused to cooperate. Nothing had worked. If he was forced to give up hope and return, there was nothing left for him. Nothing but the same bleak days and nights he'd endured before coming here.

So how could he and Alex resolve this thing between them and get back to where they'd been before that kiss?

He thought of the pleasant conversation. The easy laughter. He'd enjoyed it more than he'd realized. He wanted that again.

And he wanted her. Wanted to feast on her. Inch by tantalizing inch. It was the first thing he thought about in the morning. The last coherent thought each night. And it was making him crazy.

He bit down on an oath. Maybe that was what he wanted, but it wouldn't be right for either of them. He was in no condition for more than a casual relationship. If Alex were a different sort of woman, he'd simply enjoy a few weeks of hot sex, and get on with his life. But Alexandra Sullivan didn't strike him as the type for a brief fling, no matter how torrid. He knew, from the first time he'd looked into those eyes, that she was the kind of woman a man made promises to. Promises he'd rather die than break.

There was something else to consider. Actually, someone else. Their two grandfathers, who had been friends for more than fifty years. Those two old men wouldn't take kindly to anyone who abused that friendship.

He stood and picked up the backpack. There was plenty of time for heavy thinking on the hike back. From the looks of that sun, it would be evening before he made it back to the lodge.

Between now and then he had to come up with a way to be around Alex without trying to ravish her. Not that he didn't still want to. But he had to find a way to curb that appetite and locate some comfortable ground where the two of them could meet without all this tension.

He flashed a quick grin. What he wouldn't give, though, for just one night with Alex Sullivan. He had no doubt it would be memorable.

Chapter 6

Alex pulled on a pair of warm woolen leggings in pale oatmeal and slipped a softly cowled tunic in the same shade over her head. She was grateful for the warmth, since there had been a definite bite in the air by the time she and Lem had finished for the day. The hot shower had felt heavenly.

Humming along with the music on her stereo, she pulled the pins from her hair and ran a brush through the tangles. Then she started down the hall toward the kitchen. When she pushed open the door she was surprised to find Grant standing at the stove, stirring something in a big iron skillet.

"I thought you were still out in the woods. I didn't hear you come in."

"No wonder. When I passed your room you were singing along with the Dixie Chicks." He saw the slight flush on her cheeks. "Not bad, for a shower serenade."

She struggled to push aside the feelings of unease. He looked entirely too cool and confident. "What are you making?"

"Chili. I hope you don't mind. I found some ground sirloin in the cooler. I figured I'd get started while you were giving a concert in your room. No telling how long you intended to stand under that warm spray."

"It felt great. The temperature must have dropped twenty degrees since this afternoon."

"Yeah. I noticed. Got any grated cheese?"

"No. But I have a block of cheddar and a grater."

"Even better." He stirred the bubbling chili and turned the heat to simmer.

She rummaged in the cupboards until she located the grater. Then she began unwrapping the cheese.

He reached for it. "I'll do that…"

Her hand held firm. "I can do this…"

They both stopped, then awkwardly tried again.

"You made the chili." She lifted her chin. "The least I can do is grate the cheese."

"You worked all day, while all I did was hike." He reached a hand to hers, and noticed that she pulled away as though burned when their flesh made contact. "Okay." He turned away abruptly. "I'll start the biscuits."

"You're making biscuits?" Her fingers were still vibrating, and she struggled to regain her composure.

"Not from scratch." He pointed to the can of dough. "It says on the label that all I have to do is arrange them on a cookie tin and bake for fifteen minutes. I think I can manage that."

He began setting them on a baking sheet.

"I'm still impressed." She grated cheese into a bowl. "Most of the men who come up here to hunt wouldn't even be willing to attempt biscuits."

When the bowl was filled with cheese she turned and bumped into Grant, who was just straightening.

They jerked apart.

Flustered, Alex turned on the taps and began to wash the grater while Grant focused on placing the tin in the oven and setting the timer.

She glanced over her shoulder. "Where do you want to…?"

He turned to her at the same moment. "What do you think about…?"

They both stopped.

Grant waved a hand. "Go ahead. You first."

"No. What did you want to say?"

He turned toward the stove and stirred the chili,

then dropped the spoon with a clatter. "Look. I'm sorry about what's...happened between us. That is, I'm not sorry. In fact, I'd do it again. But I don't like what it's doing to us now. I'd like to start over."

Alex took a deep breath. "Yeah. Me, too."

"Great." For the first time he smiled. "I think I'd like a beer. How about you?"

"I'd like that."

He removed two cold beers and popped the tops, then poured one into a mug and handed it to her. He lifted a can to his lips and drank deeply. "While the chili's simmering, I'll go toss another log on the fire. That is, if you don't mind eating in the great room."

"That's fine with me." She waited until he'd sauntered from the room. Then she leaned against the counter and took a deep breath. Starting over wasn't as easy as she'd hoped. The mere touch of his hand had brought the familiar heat. But she was determined to relax and have an enjoyable evening.

If it killed her.

"When did you start working here at the lodge?" Grant settled himself in front of the roaring fire and tucked into his chili.

"Back in high school and college, Buck Thornton ran the lodge for Grandpa Sully. I used to spend my summers here, working as Buck's assistant. I'd take fishing parties out for the day, and occasionally act as trail guide when a group of hunters wanted to go up into the hills. At first Buck wasn't keen on having a girl working, even if it was only part-time. He was worried that the old-boys' club would be annoyed at the intrusion of a female in their midst. But when the others realized that I wasn't going to faint at the sight of a bloody carcass, and could actually outhike most of the hunters, they started to accept me. As he got older Buck began giving me more and more responsibility until finally he decided he was ready to retire. The timing couldn't have been more perfect. I'd just finished a stint with Grandpa Sully at Lake Como, and he was urging me to take over the operation of one of our hotels. When this became available, I knew I couldn't go anywhere else.''

She realized that she'd finished an entire bowl of chili while she'd been talking. As she spooned more into her dish, she glanced over. ''Did I remember to tell you how good this is? I want your recipe.''

''Now I'm not sure I can do that.'' He shot her a grin over the rim of his beer. ''It's an old family recipe, passed down from father to son for four generations. We Malones guard it with our lives. If I told you, I'd have to marry you, just to see that it stayed in the family.''

''Okay. But I'll have to squeeze the ceremony

in between chores. I want the lodge winterized before the first snowfall.''

"You're such a romantic," he deadpanned.

"Yeah. That's what all the guys tell me.'' She lifted the spoon to her mouth and tasted, then rolled her eyes, considering. "No. I don't think it's worth marriage. An engagement, maybe. A wild fling. But marriage…?'' She shook her head and laughed when he lifted his hands to her throat.

"All right. So the chili recipe is off-limits. Now about these biscuits…''

He leaned back and sipped his beer. "No problem. The Dough Boy tells anyone who'll listen. He probably has his own Web site.''

"Did your grandfather ever tell you about the night he ate twenty-six buttermilk biscuits?''

He lowered his beer. "You're kidding.''

"No I'm not.'' She took another bite of chili before setting aside the bowl and picking up her mug of beer. "There were six hunters here that weekend. Grandpa Sully, your grandfather and four of their cronies. They'd been trying to one-up each other the entire time. First it was the biggest fish. Everybody had to put ten dollars in the pot, knowing whoever caught the biggest would win. Mickey came close, but one of the others beat his catch by three ounces. The next day, everybody had to ante up another ten dollars before going hunting with their cameras. Grandpa Sully snagged a shot of an eight-point buck and won that jackpot. Your grandfather was getting desperate to win. And that night over poker, wouldn't you know that one of the group drew a full house.''

''Another sixty-dollar jackpot,'' Grant muttered.

''Exactly.'' Alex started chuckling. ''They were coming up on the last day, and just about everybody had won except Mickey. So, in desperation, your grandfather bet the others that he could eat more biscuits in one sitting than anybody else. One man said he could eat half a dozen. Mickey scoffed. Then Grandpa Sully said he could eat a whole dozen. Again Mickey laughed, and offered to go head-to-head, double or nothing.'' She laughed, remembering. ''You have to understand. Grandpa Sully isn't the sort of man who can ever pass up a bet if the price is right. And your grandfather knew it. So there they were, like two little boys, egging each other on. Grandpa Sully ate six, and Mickey ate seven. Grandpa Sully ate four more and Mickey matched him. All around the table, the others were taunting them like a pack of bullies. Grandpa Sully managed ten more, then watched as Mickey gulped down eleven without even swallowing them. That did it. Grandpa Sully ate five more before he started to turn green, and Mickey matched him. Then Mickey calmly ate one more, licked the crumbs from the plate, and watched while my grandfather counted out one hundred and twenty dollars. A minute later Mickey rushed out of the room, while everybody sat around howling. We figured he was going to pay dearly for that jackpot.''

Grant shook his head from side to side while he roared with laughter. "Leave it to my grandfather. But at least he'd earned bragging rights for another year."

"Yep. It's wonderful to watch those two together. They've had such great times through the years." She got to her feet. "Want another beer?"

"Sure."

While she was gone, Grant tossed a log on the fire, and stood watching as the flames began to lick along the bark. It occurred to him that he hadn't laughed this much in a year. It felt good. Everything about this night felt good. Being here with Alex Sullivan. Doing nothing more important than swapping stories of their grandfathers' escapades and enjoying the warmth of a fire.

"Here you are." She handed him another beer.

As their fingers brushed, they both took a step back and realized that the spark was still there. But at least they recognized it for what it was, and were able to hold it at bay.

For the time being.

Alex had curled up in one corner of the sofa, her feet tucked beneath her. "Mickey once told me he was a retired police captain."

"Yeah. One of New York's finest."

She heard the note of pride in his tone. "Through the years I've heard a number of his stories."

"Yeah, that's my grandfather. He has a million of them. I grew up hearing his tales of heroes and villains. I couldn't get enough of them. I used to spend my weekends with him just so I could listen to him and his wild tales. In his day, the cops were always the good guys. And the good guys always won."

"That's the way it's supposed to be."

"Yeah." He stood and poked at the fire until the charred log flared into flame. Then he returned the poker to the fire set and remained where he was, staring into the flames as though mesmerized.

Alex studied the way he looked. His eyes slightly narrowed. His thumbs hooked into his pockets. Where did he go when he lapsed into silence? Wherever it was, he didn't go willingly. There was a pensiveness, a sadness that tugged at her heart.

Except for his grandfather, Grant mentioned no family. And though she was curious, she was reluctant to probe. When he was ready, he would talk about himself and those he loved. Until then, she'd stick to safe, bland topics that wouldn't stir up unhappy memories.

"Lem says it'll snow by the end of the week."

He lifted his head. Pulled himself back from his thoughts. "How does he know?"

"His knee. It's his weather barometer. He always knows days before it rains or snows. Or whenever the weather is about to make a drastic change."

"Think he's more accurate than the TV weathercasters, with all their maps and charts?"

"Absolutely."

"Then he ought to patent it. He could retire from this job and make himself a fortune."

Alex laughed. "That wouldn't even tempt Lem. He's been working here at the lodge for more than fifty years. Even when he held a second job, he used to come by just to lend a hand. It was never for the money. It still isn't. Snug Harbor Lodge is his second home."

"That's obvious. He takes a lot of pride in his work. And it shows. I don't think I've ever seen tools that old gleam like new."

Alex laughed. "He polishes them as soon as he's finished with them."

"I believe it. And that shed." Grant shook his head. "You could eat off the workbench."

"I wouldn't recommend it. There have been some pretty unappetizing specimens found there."

They shared a laugh.

Grant held up the empty can. "I think I've had enough of this. How about some coffee?"

"Sure thing." Before she could get up he shook his head.

"You stay where you are. I'll make it."

He returned a short time later with a tray of coffee and cups. After pouring, he handed one to Alex and helped himself to the other, before walking to the window to peer out at the darkness.

"When did Lem say we'd get that snow?"

"He didn't say. He just told me it would be here before the week was out."

"He was right on the money. Look."

Alex hurried over to switch on the outside lights, revealing a curtain of snow.

"Oh." She clasped her hands together and pressed her nose to the window to stare in silence.

Grant was watching her reaction. "You don't seem very unhappy about this."

She shook her head, sending her hair dancing around her shoulders. "I can't help myself. I always feel like a kid when I see the first snowfall of the season. It's just so beautiful."

"Yeah." And so was she. He clenched his hand into a fist at his side to keep from touching her. "Did Lem say how much snow would fall?"

"Just a dusting. But it's a start." She breathed deeply. "I need to get at the rest of those tree limbs tomorrow. Wouldn't want them crashing down in a storm.''

''I'll give you a hand.''

She turned to smile at him. ''You don't need to do that. Lem will be here.''

''I want to. I've had enough tramping through the woods alone. Besides, I think I'd like to spend an entire day with the two of you, just to see how many words the old guy can string together into one sentence.''

She laughed. ''You'd be surprised. Sometimes he can be downright talkative.''

''Uh-huh.'' He grinned, and Alex thought again how appealing he was when he was relaxed. ''You're not fooling me. I've already concluded that the two of you communicate through telepathy.''

''Another secret revealed.'' She gave a mock sigh. ''Next thing you know, people will discover how wonderful this place can be in winter, when it's covered by six feet of snow. And then my winter hibernation will come to a close and I'll have to endure the rigors of success.''

''Hey. It could be worse. You could be up here all alone and begging for visitors.'' He found himself tugging on a lock of her hair before he realized what he was doing. At once he felt the rush of heat, and saw a similar blaze in her eyes.

For the space of several moments they merely stared at each other in silence.

Grant didn't know which was worse. Having to ignore the hunger he could read in her eyes. Or having to deny the needs that had his throat dry and his heart pumping furiously.

He'd made himself a promise. And for as long as he could manage it, he intended to tough it out.

He lowered his hand and took a step back.

"Well, this has been great." He turned away and started across the room, forcing a lightness to his tone he didn't feel. "Now if you don't mind, Ms. Sullivan, since I did the cooking, I'll leave the cleaning to you while I retire to my room."

"I don't mind at all, Mr. Malone. Cleaning is my life." She followed his example and kept her words light. "Good night."

"'Night."

"See you in the morning."

"Yeah. See you."

She waited until she heard the door to his room close. Then she poured herself a second cup of coffee and returned to the window to watch the snowflakes dance past.

She was proud of the fact that they'd managed to get through the entire evening without giving in to whatever feelings were there just below the surface. But the truth was, it had been much more difficult than she'd anticipated. Instead of the situation being better, she had the sense that it was actually much worse.

They'd kept things from boiling over this time. But sooner or later, she feared all those simmering feelings would simply explode. And when they did, she'd be helpless to do more than hold on and ride out the storm.

Chapter 7

"Well? Are you happy?" Grant pointed to the window, where early morning sunlight glinted off a ground dusted with snow.

"Oh, it's lovely." Alex paused to admire the view.

While she did, he took the moment to study her. She looked as fresh and radiant as a kid at Christmas in sturdy denims and a turtleneck. Her hair was tied back with a strip of plain leather. Her complexion, free of makeup, was, as always, flawless.

She turned away from the window. It occurred to her that this was the first time she'd seen him this early in the morning. "What do you usually eat for breakfast?"

"Breakfast? What's that?"

"The meal we eat in the morning, to get our body jump-started for the day."

"Oh. That. I usually eat whatever is in my refrigerator, as long as it isn't moving or covered with mold."

"Good. You're easy." She opened the pantry and removed several boxes of cereal. "There's milk and juice in the fridge."

While Grant retrieved them, she started grinding fresh coffee beans. By the time they sat down to bowls of cereal topped with slices of bananas and peaches, Alex had poured two steaming cups of coffee.

He tasted, then sighed. "Home was never like this."

"All it takes is a little planning and a little shopping." She poured milk from a pitcher into her bowl. "Neither of which I can really admit to. I have this wonderful neighbor who fills my larder during my busy season. She and her daughters help with the cooking, cleaning and laundry. I haven't seen them now for over a week. But I expect she'll be stopping by in the next day or so with a supply of goodies from the village market."

"Nice. If I had a friendly shopper, that would take care of the food. But what would I do about the woman across the table?"

"There are plenty of those around." She sipped her coffee. "Have you ever been married?"

"No."

"I'm surprised." She studied him over the rim of her cup. "Haven't you even been tempted?"

He nodded. "A time or two. But most women aren't interested when they learn what line of work…" He paused, then simply picked up his cup and drank.

For long moments there was a strained silence. Finally, he said, "How about you, Alex? Ever been married?"

She shook her head.

"Ever come close?"

She smiled, remembering. "Once. Fortunately for both of us, I came to my senses in time."

"Why do you say that?"

"He hated the country. Thought hiking in the mountains was for nature freaks. Absolutely loathed snow and cold. His idea of a good time was following the sun and surf from one coast to the other. He paid his way by doing odd jobs, then moving on before he could grow bored with what he called 'the worker drones' of life. Can you imagine a more unlikely mate?"

Grant was chuckling. "The two of you must have had something in common. What attracted you to him in the first place?"

She finished her cereal and carried the empty

bowl to the sink. "If you must know, he looked great in a bathing suit. And I was a shallow eighteen-year-old."

"Oh, that explains it. Are you telling me that now that you've matured, you no longer look at guys in bathing suits?"

"I didn't say that." She rinsed the bowl and set it in the dishwasher. "I may be ten years older now, but I'm nobody's fool. I still like a great body." She closed the door of the dishwasher and straightened.

She strolled to the door. "I hear Lem's truck. You can find us out in the shed when you're finished with breakfast."

He watched as the door closed behind her. Then he grinned as he bent to his cereal.

By the time Grant finished breakfast and made his way outside, Alex was standing on a ladder, a chainsaw in her hand. While he watched she cut through a tree limb, sending it crashing to the ground. Minutes later she dropped a second branch, before descending the ladder.

While she dragged the ladder to another tree, Lem began hauling the branches toward the side of the lodge.

"What'll you do with these?" Grant asked.

"Firewood." The old man pointed to a pile of logs neatly stacked against the wall.

"You sure you need more?"

Lem nodded. "Alex'll go through a couple cords this winter."

"Okay." Grant picked up a long-handled ax, testing its weight. "I'll handle these. That way you can give Alex a hand over there."

The old man grunted his approval and walked away.

It was several hours later before Alex and Lem put away the ladder and saw and began cleaning up the debris. The sudden silence was punctuated with the sound of an ax biting into wood. Alex was surprised to see Grant working his way through a mountain of firewood. On his face was a look of extreme concentration, as though the logs were his enemies and he was deriving a great deal of satisfaction out of destroying them slowly, piece by piece.

She walked closer. He'd removed his parka and rolled the sleeves of his flannel shirt. As he lifted the ax high over his head, then brought it down to bite cleanly through another log, she felt her throat go dry at the ripple of muscles.

"I'm glad to see you enjoy chopping wood."

His head came up. For the space of a moment he merely stared at her with eyes that were so hot and fierce, she found herself taking a step back. Then he blinked, and she wondered if she'd only imagined that look.

He managed a smile. "This is a great workout. Better than a gym."

She relaxed. "Well, I'm glad to hear you say that. Then you won't mind spending the rest of the week cutting up these logs into firewood?"

"I might be interested. What's it worth to you, Ms. Sullivan?"

"You want payment?" She thought a moment. "How about a tender pot roast with all the trimmings, served in front of a roaring fire?"

"Add cherry pie and you've got yourself a deal."

"Cherry pie?" She was frowning when she heard the sound of tires crunching gravel.

She turned to see a bright red van pulling up beside Lem's truck. A woman and two girls stepped out, all carrying bags of groceries.

"Hi there, Alex," the woman called cheerfully. "I figured by now you'd be running low on supplies."

Alex laughed. "My hero. If you brought the fixings for a cherry pie, I just might cut a deal here."

"Cherry pie?" The woman turned to one of her daughters. "Kayla, go look in that other bag in the van. I've got cherry and blueberry filling."

The girl danced off, then returned holding up a can. Alex took it and gave her a hug. "Looks like I'm going to have enough firewood to last me the winter. And all it's costing me is this."

Grant leaned on his ax. "I think you've forgotten the pot roast and all the trimmings."

"I haven't forgotten. That's what I was going to fix tonight anyway." She turned to include the others. "Grant Malone, this is Bren Trainor and her daughters Kayla and Kelsey."

Grant gave them his best smile. "It's a pleasure meeting you. Alex tells me you're the ones who supply all the fine food we've been enjoying."

"So much food," Alex added, "I probably won't get through it until next spring."

Bren dimpled. She was a pretty woman with a short blond bob and sky blue eyes. "Well, the way you work, I figure you need plenty of protein. Besides, I have to shop for myself, so I may as well pick up a few things for you."

"A few things?" Alex peered into Kelsey's bag. "Steaks, chops and is that a turkey?"

"Just a little one. They were having a special at Benson's Market."

"Uh-huh." Alex grinned. "Come on inside. We'll put these things away and you can stay for lunch."

"Only if you let us do something. We thought while we were here we'd change the bed linens and do a couple of loads of laundry."

Alex dropped an arm around the woman's shoulders and called to Grant, "See why I love them?"

When they were safely indoors, the two girls,

aged fourteen and fifteen, dropped their groceries and ran to the window to watch as Grant returned to his chore.

"What are you two doing?" their mother called.

The two girls looked at each other and began giggling, before turning back to the window. As Alex paused beside them, Kayla, the older of the two asked, "How long is Grant staying?"

"He hasn't said. Why?"

"Why?" The girl rolled her eyes, then began giggling again. "He's better looking than a movie star."

Her sister nodded. "An absolute hunk." She turned to Alex. "You mean you haven't noticed?"

Alex grinned. "Oh, I've noticed." She started out of the room. "Bren, if you put the groceries away, I'll strip the beds and bring the towels and linens to the laundry room."

"The girls can do that." Bren protested.

Alex shook her head. "I don't mind. Besides, they're too busy staring at the incredible hunk."

The four shared a knowing laugh before Alex headed down the hall. Behind her she could hear Bren calling her girls to help her put away the groceries or, she threatened, she'd lower the blinds.

Alex was still laughing when she walked into Grant's room. After tossing all his towels into a pile in the middle of the hallway, she returned to strip the bed. It gave her a strange feeling to think about that hard, muscled body stretched out on these sheets. There was that flutter again in the pit of her stomach. It annoyed her even while it caused the most pleasant of sensations. She knew she was behaving much like Kayla and Kelsey. Instead of standing with her nose pressed to the window to watch him, she carried his image in her mind. And whenever she allowed herself to think of him, it was always the same. The flutter of her pulse. The dry throat. And the incredible feeling. She pressed her hand to her stomach.

As she paused beside the bed, she caught sight of the open drawer of Grant's night table. For the space of a heartbeat she froze, unable to breathe.

Glinting in the afternoon sunlight was a very small, very deadly looking pistol.

Grant was feeling mellow. This hard, demanding work was just what he'd been craving. The long hikes up into the hills had been a start. He'd found solace in the quiet, pristine forest. And pleasure in the exploration of the primitive environment that surrounded the lodge. But this was infinitely more satisfying. While punishing his muscles, and pushing himself to the limit physically, he was also able to lose himself in thought. With every bite of blade into wood he felt a measure of satisfaction.

He paused to wipe his arm across his forehead. The afternoon sun had melted the snow, leaving only a few traces beneath evergreens. When he looked up Alex was striding toward him. On her face was a look he hadn't seen before.

When she opened her hand, his eyes narrowed with sudden fury.

"What the hell were you doing in my room?"

"I'll ask the questions here." The cool, controlled tone of her voice alerted Lem, who walked up to stand beside her like a mute bodyguard.

"What were you thinking, bringing a gun like this to my lodge?"

"It's my gun. I have a right to carry it. Would you like to see my permit?"

"I don't care about a piece of paper. I know guns. This isn't a hunting rifle. As far as I can see, there's only one purpose for a handgun like this. And it's to kill people."

"Or to protect people from being killed." His tone was pure ice.

"Is that why you brought this here? To protect me? Or maybe Lem?" Her voice hardened. "Or are you the one who needs protection? Because if you do, you ought to be carrying it on your person, instead of leaving it where an innocent young girl could have come upon it."

"All right." He stuck out his hand. "I'll keep it with me."

She snatched her hand back. "Just a minute. You asked what I was doing in your room. I was stripping your bed. And you can be thankful I was the one who took on that chore. It could have been Kayla or Kelsey who found this."

He blanched. His tone softened. "Look. I've never been careless with my weapons. But I thought you and I would be alone up here." He glanced at Lem, who continued to stand beside Alex. On the old man's face was a look that told Grant, better than any words, that he'd do whatever it took to protect her. "I'm sorry. I can see that I owe you an explanation. I'm a New York City cop. Or was, until I took a...leave."

She should have known. The lean, taut body. The hard edge she'd seen in those eyes. Eyes that seemed to be constantly searching his surroundings. As though expecting to find trouble at every turn.

His tone lowered. "I came up here for a much-needed rest."

She kept her own voice unemotional. "But you brought your gun."

"That's not so unusual for a police officer. In the city, I never go anywhere without my gun."

Anger crept into her tone. "You're not in the city now. As long as you're here, I want this gun locked up with the hunting rifles. Unless you agree to that, you'll have to leave here at once."

She saw something flicker in his eyes, and knew that it couldn't be easy for a man like Grant to comply with such orders. For the space of several seconds he seemed to consider the consequences.

It occurred to him that when he'd first arrived here, he'd seen danger behind every tree. A threat lurking behind every boulder. It was a measure of how far he'd come that he was able to finally nod his agreement.

"I can live with that."

"Good." She handed it to him, causing Lem to blink in surprise. "I'd like you to check your weapon and see that it's properly unloaded. Then you can come with me and watch while I secure it and the ammunition in a padlocked cabinet."

He cradled the gun in his hand with an ease that sent prickles along her scalp. Though she'd grown up with rifles, and was comfortable around hunters, this gun and the man who was casually removing its bullets, seemed completely alien to her.

When the gun was emptied, she led Grant into the lodge and up the stairs to the gallery overlooking the great room. The wall was made of narrow panels of aged oak. When Alex pressed the first panel, it opened to reveal a padlocked cabinet hidden behind it. From a ring of keys Alex produced one that opened the lock. Inside was a custom rack holding more than a dozen rifles of various calibers.

Grant ran a hand lightly over them. Each had

been carefully oiled, with the proper ammunition resting on a shelf just below. "I'm impressed."

"Grandpa Sully figured that a hunting lodge might be a logical place for a thief to break into if he were bent on stealing weapons. So he didn't want to make it easy by storing them in a conspicuous place."

"I'll give your grandfather high marks. This is clever."

She indicated a shelf. "You can put your gun and bullets there."

He set them down, then took a step back. Alex locked the cabinet, and returned the wood panel to its proper position, completely concealing the cabinet behind it.

She turned away before glancing over her shoulder to see him keeping pace just behind her. "In case you're wondering, I have the only key. You'll get your gun back when you're ready to leave."

He nodded. "Fair enough."

But as he followed her along the upper gallery, he found himself looking back at the cabinet, and already missing the comfort of his gun. However much he might tell himself that he was far enough from the city to relax, it simply wasn't in his nature. Besides, common sense told him that even here in this serene, untouched wilderness, there was no such thing as complete safety.

As he descended the stairs, he was already second-guessing himself. He hoped he wouldn't live to regret this decision. But the simple truth was his desire to stay here with this woman had become even stronger than his need for his weapon.

That wasn't an easy admission for him to make. But it was time for some honesty. Something was happening to him. Something completely beyond his control.

He was beginning to care far too much about Alex Sullivan.

Chapter 8

"Okay, girls." Bren looked up from the stove, where she was stirring a pot of steaming soup. "You can tell Alex and the men that lunch is ready."

"I'll go get Grant." Kayla, older by a year, turned to Kelsey. "You can call Alex and Lem."

"Oh, no you don't." Kelsey raced to the door ahead of her. "*I'll* get Grant. You get the others."

"Mom!" Kayla was shouting at the top of her lungs when she dashed after her younger sister and shot off the porch without even using the steps.

As the door slammed behind them, Bren stood watching through the window, shaking her head. Both girls were ogling Grant as he brought the ax down on another log, splitting it in two.

It seemed to their mother that it took forever before her daughters tore themselves away from the hunk to summon Alex and Lem to lunch.

A short time later they were all seated at the kitchen table enjoying thick ham and cheese sandwiches and bowls of corn chowder.

"Oh, Bren." Alex sighed over the food. "You're a lifesaver. I didn't realize just how hungry I was until now."

The two men were too busy eating to say a word. They each devoured several sandwiches and nearly inhaled the soup. When Grant finally leaned back with a cup of coffee, he didn't even notice the two teenagers watching him.

But Alex did, and had to hide her smile behind her napkin.

"Do you work for Alex?" Kayla asked.

Grant shook his head. "Nope. I'm just a guest."

"You are? How come you're doing all that work?" This from Kelsey.

"I like to work. Especially if I get to work up a sweat."

The two girls stared at his flannel shirt, plastered to his chest, and sighed in unison.

Kayla's eyes were glinting with excitement. "How long will you be staying here?"

Alex could already see those teenage wheels in motion. Kayla was wondering if Grant would still be here when she and her sister started back to work in the spring.

Grant shrugged. "I'm not sure. I guess as long as Alex and I can stand each other's company. I figure one of these days she'll tell me to pack up and get going."

The two girls looked from Grant to Alex, then back. It occurred to Alex that the man seated across the table, who had already turned to Lem to ask about sharpening the ax, didn't have a clue as to what these two were thinking. She tried to see Grant through their eyes, and realized that he was indeed better looking than a movie star. He had a tragic look about him that made a woman want to offer comfort. His eyes were dark, hooded, hiding a hundred secrets. But when he focused them on someone, he was able to concentrate all his attention. It was as though everyone and everything else disappeared. His face had a chiseled, rugged look that made a woman's heart flutter. But it was softened by a poet's mouth. And when he gave one of those rare smiles, no one was immune. At least that was the effect it had on her. Add to that six feet of the most perfectly sculpted body, and it was easy to see why two teenage girls had just lost their hearts.

Hadn't she already lost hers?

She pushed away from the table. "That was a

great lunch, Bren. I've got my energy back. Now it's time to tackle the rest of those trees."

As she pulled on her parka, Bren called, "The girls and I will finish up in here. And if you'd like, I'll get that roast started before I leave."

"You're a saint, Bren. Thanks."

Alex nearly ran out the door. What she needed was fresh air to clear her head. And an afternoon of bone-jarring chores to work off whatever fool-ishness was suddenly taking over her common sense.

Lem stood in the back of his truck, rolling out the logs he'd collected from beneath the trees.

Bren and her girls had left more than an hour ago. But not until both Kayla and Kelsey had stood around watching Grant chop wood until their mother had been forced to catch them by the arms and drag them to the car.

"I'm running out of space here, Lem." Grant paused beside the rear wall of the lodge, piled neatly with logs all the way to the roof. "Where would you like a second stack?"

"How about between those two trees?" The older man pointed to a clear section nearby.

"Fine. I'll get at it."

Lem rolled out the last of the logs, before jumping down to stand beside the truck. "You sure you want to tackle any more of this today? You've managed to accomplish what it usually takes Alex and me a month or more to do.''

Grant smiled at the compliment. ''May as well get it done.''

''Okay. I can see that your muscles are up to it. Just wondering about your hands. Most cops I know don't spend their days swinging an ax.''

Grant lifted his palms and could see the blisters already forming. ''Yeah. You're right. I guess I should have built up to this slowly.'' He glanced over. ''Got any gloves I can borrow?''

''In the shed. First drawer on the left in the workbench. Take the ones with padded leather palms.''

''Thanks, Lem.''

When he returned the older man was already cleaning up the debris around the first stack. While he raked, Grant began chopping. Soon the two men had fallen into a comfortable rhythm of chopping, stacking and raking. After another hour they paused and settled themselves on a couple of stumps, enjoying a break in the routine in the clear frigid air.

Lem removed a pipe from his pocket and took his time filling the bowl before holding a match to it.

Grant watched as smoke wreathed his head. ''This is a great place to work.''

''Yep.''

"Alex says you've been here for over fifty years."

The old man nodded. "Watched this place grow from a private hunting lodge to a guest lodge. And got a chance to watch Alex grow from girl to woman."

Grant looked across the clearing, where Alex, having removed all the dead limbs from nearby trees, was now oiling and cleaning the chainsaw. "She's amazing. Is there anything she can't do?"

Lem shook his head. "Can't think of anything offhand. Except maybe enjoy herself at fancy parties. She's more at home hiking up into the hills."

The two men shared a laugh.

"I'm not much for fancy parties myself." Grant idly drew off the gloves to examine his blisters.

"You have to go to many up there in the city?"

"A few." He frowned. "Once or twice a year the mayor likes to toss celebrities and city employees together for award ceremonies. I've attended enough that I had to buy a tux."

Lem peered at him through a haze of smoke, as a half-forgotten memory began to stir in his mind. "You one of those who got an award?"

"Yeah." Grant spat the word as though it offended him.

"What for?"

"Nothing much." Annoyed, he stood and drew

on the gloves. "Think I'll tackle a couple more logs."

Lem watched in silence, then tapped the glowing tobacco from his pipe and ground it into the dirt with his booted heel before tucking the pipe into his pocket.

"Got some errands to run for Alex up in the village. After that I'll be heading home. Going to call it a day."

"See you tomorrow," Grant called.

The old man nodded and made his way to the shed where Alex was stowing her tools. "Going into town now. I'll pick up that fuel oil you wanted. Need anything else?"

She looked up. "No thanks, Lem. That's all I need."

He motioned toward Grant, who brought the ax down with such force the pieces flew through the air. "I'd say he's determined to earn that cherry pie."

"The pie." She gave a pained expression. "I can't believe I got suckered into that. Now I'm going to have to go inside and become a domestic goddess, like my sister, Lizbeth."

The old man was grinning as he made his way to his truck. But once inside his smile faded. As he put the truck in gear, he began mulling over all Grant had revealed.

* * *

It took nearly two hours for Grant to work off his frustration. Just talking about the mayor's party, and the presentation in front of hundreds of dignitaries, had unleashed all the demons. But now, as he made his way to the shed, he was relieved that his good nature had been restored. He hung the ax on a hook along one wall, before returning the padded gloves to their drawer. Once again he was struck by the simple order of things here at the lodge. Whether it was inside, with its padlocked rifle storage and thoroughly stocked pantry, or out here in the toolshed, with its perfect symmetry of hooks, shelves and drawers, everything had its place. And it was expected that everything would be returned to that place when the job was done. Grant glanced at the wooden sign hanging above the doorway. It was a source of pride for both Alex and Lem. Well-deserved pride, he thought.

He stepped out and latched the door before turning to stare at the lake. Darkness had begun to settle over the land, and the sunset was reflected in the still water.

There was such a natural order to life out here. Morning, with its chorus of birds and the mist rising off the lake as the sun came up. Afternoon, with that thin winter light easing the bite in the air. And at twilight, those last rays glinting behind the wooded peaks of the distant hills, casting the lodge and the surrounding low-lying area in shadow.

When he stepped into the lodge, he breathed in the mouthwatering fragrance of pot roast and began to salivate. As he made his way down the hall to his room, he found himself wondering if Alex had actually baked that cherry pie. He showered and dressed quickly, eager to find out.

When he passed the great room, he paused. In the glow of the fire he could see that the coffee table had been set with gleaming china, crystal and silver. When he stepped into the kitchen, he paused in the doorway to admire the view.

Alex was wearing a cheery red sweater and narrow black denims that displayed her slender form to its best advantage. She'd left her hair long and loose and it fell in a curtain over one eye as she bent to the oven to remove a tray of steaming rolls. As she set them on the counter, she caught sight of him and felt the familiar flutter around her heart.

Why did he have to look so handsome? His dark hair glistened with drops of water from the shower. The charcoal cords and sweater added to his rugged looks.

"Is that a cherry pie?"

She gave him a haughty look. "You mean you didn't expect me to live up to my half of the bargain?"

"I just didn't expect you to find the time."

"Well, I had to let a few chores go. But it was worth it. From the looks of that woodpile, I'll have enough firewood to last through next spring." She motioned toward a bottle of wine. "Would you mind pouring?"

He lifted the bottle, read the label, and arched a brow. "Is this a celebration?"

"I thought this dinner deserved something special."

He filled two tulip glasses and handed one to her. The touch of her hand brought the usual heat, and he itched to touch more. "Here's to a very satisfying day."

She smiled. "It was, wasn't it?"

He tasted, nodded. "We got a lot done. And if a blizzard should come roaring through tonight, you won't have to worry about any branches crashing through the roof."

"Lem says the first big snowfall should happen within the week."

He couldn't help chuckling. "The old knee forecast, huh?"

"Yes. And I put more faith in that than in our weathercasters." She handed him her glass. "If you'll carry this to the other room, I'll just put those rolls in a basket and bring in dinner."

"I'll get the cart."

"Not tonight. I'm going to serve you. Not that

I intend to do it more than once. But I want you to know that I always pay my debts.''

He grinned. ''A guy could get used to this.''

''Don't worry. You might never see it again. So enjoy.''

He was still smiling as he picked up the bottle of wine and walked to the great room. While he topped off their glasses, Alex wheeled the serving cart to the coffee table and began to serve their plates.

After just one bite Grant sighed with pure pleasure. ''I haven't tasted pot roast this tender since I was a kid and my grandmother used to make it every Sunday.''

''My grandmother used to ask the chef to prepare prime rib for special Sunday dinners.''

He chuckled. ''See how much we have in common?''

They both roared with laughter.

''Actually...'' He took another bite and closed his eyes in enjoyment.

''Actually what?''

He chewed, swallowed. ''I don't think you can take credit for this. Didn't Bren say she'd get it started?''

''That's right. But I was the one who peeled the potatoes, and added carrots and little pearl onions and my favorite vegetable, turnips.''

He glanced at the side dish with a look of disdain. "You're kidding. Nobody likes turnips."

"Aha. I see you haven't tasted mine. Here. One bite and you'll be hooked."

He dipped a fork into something that resembled mashed potatoes. He tasted, swallowed, then gave her a look of complete surprise. "This is wonderful. But I don't believe it's turnips. What's really in it?"

"I mash turnips with butter and garlic, a little salt and pepper. That's all."

"That's all?" He helped himself to more while she merely smiled.

"See there? Another convert. It happens every time." She picked up her wine and sipped while he polished off everything on his plate and went back for seconds.

He glanced at her plate. "You're through?"

She nodded. "While you were showering I cheated and nibbled the whole time I was getting everything ready. Now I'm paying the price."

He merely laughed. "More for me."

"Was that an oink I heard?"

"Yeah. But I worked up a mean appetite cutting all that wood." He lifted the wine bottle and refilled their glasses, then leaned back, satisfied. "I was noticing how peaceful and still the lake gets just at sundown. It's really a picture. Especially with a flock of geese flying overhead."

She nodded. "You should see it in the dead of winter, when the lake freezes and everything is covered with snow. The air is so cold it hurts to breathe it in. And you can hike for miles without seeing another human footprint."

He watched her as she turned to stare into the firelight, and wondered if she knew just how beautiful she was.

"I once sat on a stump and saw a herd of deer step into the clearing. They passed by close enough to touch, and completely ignored me as they foraged. It was such a special moment I was moved to tears. And I found myself wishing there was someone there to share it with me." She ducked her head and looked down into her glass when she realized what she'd just revealed.

Until this moment, it had never occurred to her that she missed having someone to share such moments. Until Grant's arrival, she'd never before had anyone here during her off-season. And though she valued her privacy, there had often been little twinges of loneliness. There had been books she'd read, that she'd wanted to share. Moments of beauty, or sadness or happiness that would have meant more if there'd been someone there to experience them with her.

She'd expected to resent having him here. Instead, she found herself looking forward to the start of each new day.

She scrambled to her feet. "I promised you cherry pie."

While she was gone, Grant stared at the fire without really seeing it. All he could think of was the wistful tone of her voice when she'd spoken of her loneliness. It had touched something inside him. Something he'd been fighting for such a long time.

Alex returned with two slices of pie, still warm from the oven and topped with vanilla ice cream.

Grant took the first bite, then set down his fork and turned to her with a look of ecstasy. "Miss Sullivan, I think I have to marry you."

"Of course you do. All the men say that." She took her first bite and nodded with satisfaction. "Not half bad."

"You mean you've done better?"

"Many times. But that's why I'll have to refuse your generous offer of marriage, Mr. Grant. I can't allow my extraordinary skills in the kitchen to lure you into my trap. You see, besides all my many talents, I have some terrible flaws that you ought to be aware of."

"You mean you're an ax murderer?"

"Worse." She lowered her voice to a whisper. "I'm a lousy speller. I never could remember when it was *e* before *i,* and *i* before *e.* And history. I hated memorizing all those dates of battles and the names of generals."

He polished off his pie and picked up his wine. "All right. As long as we're playing truth or dare, I have a confession of my own to make. I was a prodigy. Absolutely brilliant. But I did have trouble with calculus."

"Calculus. That's all?"

"Uh-huh. Everything else was a snap."

She could see the laughter lurking in those dark eyes and decided to play along. "All right, Mr. Genius. Calculate this. If one person can clear away the dishes in half an hour, how much time will it take two people, working side by side, to do the same job?"

"Exactly five minutes."

"And how did you arrive at that?"

"I'm going to load everything onto this serving cart and put the dishes in the washer in the fastest time possible, while you cut a second slice of that fabulous pie."

"I should have known there would be food involved in this equation."

"Exactly." He shocked her by dragging her close and pressing his mouth to hers in a hard fast kiss that spun crazily through her mind, wiping away every coherent thought.

His eyes narrowed as he watched hers widen in surprise. "I've been wanting to do that since I first walked into the kitchen tonight." And a whole lot more. But he'd satisfy himself with a kiss for now.

She was forced to hold on to him so she wouldn't fall. "So why did you wait so long?"

"I wanted to be fortified with pot roast first. And now that I'm feeling..." he lowered his voice to an imitation of Boris Badinoff "...strong like bull, I think I'd like to try that again."

He was trying to keep the moment light. But this time, he framed her face and kept his eyes steady on hers as he drew her close and kissed her, long and slow and deep. She couldn't think. Could barely breathe as he drew out every taste, every flavor. It was, she thought, the same pleasure he took from eating. Except that he magnified it a hundred times or more. She could feel his lips brushing hers. Soft. So soft. And yet, despite the softness, her blood heated and her heartbeat began to pulse at her temples.

He drew her closer, until their bodies were brushing. Just enough that her breasts tingled from the contact. And still he kept his mouth light on hers. Teasing. Feathering her lips until she wanted to drag him to her and feast. But she couldn't move. All she could do was stand there, helpless as his teeth scraped lightly over her lower lip.

She couldn't stop the sound that escaped her throat. A purr of pleasure as his tongue traced the outline of her mouth before dipping inside to taste.

She was so sweet. It was a sweetness he'd never hoped to find. And now that he had, he couldn't get enough. He wanted to fill himself with her. He had the insane idea that if he were to fill himself with all this goodness, all this light, it could push aside all the darkness that had been festering for so long in his soul.

He loved feeling her melt into him. Loved the way her skin seemed to soften and warm under his touch. The way her heartbeat thundered inside her chest, matching his own. If he could, he'd go on holding her like this, kissing her like this, until they were both beyond stopping.

It was the little moan of distress that had him lifting his head and taking a step back.

"Sorry." He kept his hands on her shoulders, though he wasn't certain if he did it for her sake or his. "I keep forgetting that we weren't going to do that."

"Yeah." The single word was breathy.

"Sure you wouldn't like to try again?"

She forced a smile as she pushed away. She needed to escape before she did something foolish. Like beg him to take her right here. Right now. They were traveling a very slippery slope that was bound to knock them both off balance. "No seconds on my kisses."

"Just my luck. Okay. I'll just have to settle for pie. And then we're going to polish off the last of this wine while the fire burns low. And if you're very lucky, I'll amaze you with my…math skills."

Her laughter, smooth as velvet, washed over him and wrapped itself around his heart.

"I can hardly wait." She helped him load the cart, and was surprised that she could continue to function even though she was still vibrating with need.

Chapter 9

Grant lay a minute listening to the sounds of the morning. It had been such a long time since he'd been able to sleep through the night and wake feeling rested and refreshed.

He and Alex had talked until nearly midnight. And though there had been several times when he'd had to wage a terrible battle within himself, he'd managed considerable restraint.

What he found most amazing was the fun they'd had together, even though they'd done nothing more than talk and laugh. Along with a good bit of teasing.

He heard the door to her room open and close; heard the sound of her footsteps along the hall. He slipped out of bed, looking forward to the day.

Suddenly he stopped in midstride. How long had it been since he'd looked forward instead of backward? He was definitely making progress.

"'Morning." Lem was standing in the kitchen, enjoying a cup of coffee. "How're the hands?"

"Fine." Grant glanced at his palms. "A few blisters, but that's to be expected."

"Blisters? Why didn't you tell me this last night?" Alex turned from the pantry where she was sorting through the cereals. "I keep a complete first aid kit stocked for my guests. Let me get it."

"There's no need..." His words faded as she hurried from the room with a look of concern.

He glanced at Lem, who shrugged. "When you're my age, son, you'll realize there's no sense arguing with a female bent on doing what she thinks is best for you."

"Whether you need it or not?"

"Doesn't matter." The old man grinned. "It's what's best for her."

Minutes later Alex returned and set a plastic container on the table. After rummaging through it, she held up a vial. "It says on the label that this ointment will have your blisters healed within twenty-four hours."

Grant couldn't resist teasing. "If it can't do the job in twenty-three hours, I'm not interested."

"Oh, yes you are. Hold still." She squeezed the ointment onto his palms. "This will only burn for a minute."

"Burn?" Too late he yanked his hands away and swore under his breath.

"Excuse me." She returned the vial to the kit and arched one haughty brow as she turned to look at him. "Did you say something?"

He glowered at her. "You did that on purpose."

"Did what?"

"Poured acid on my flesh."

"Stop acting like a baby. It's just a little salve. I warned you it would burn."

"For a minute. You said a minute." He looked at Lem. "You heard her, didn't you?"

The old man was watching them with such intensity, it took him a moment to answer. It occurred to him that these two were acting a lot like an old married couple.

He drank the last of his coffee and placed his cup in the sink. "I think I'll head on outside. When you two are ready to quit sparring and get to work, you'll find me in the shed."

"I was ready to work." Grant held his hands out in front of them and shook them to stop the stinging. "Now I'm wondering how I'll be able to hold on to an ax."

"Here." Alex filled a bowl with cereal and milk

and added strawberries, as Lem let himself out. "Maybe food will soothe the beast."

Grant put a hand over hers, and lowered his voice, stopping her in her tracks. "If it's the beast in me you want to soothe, I have a much better way."

Before she could stop him his hands were on her shoulders, drawing her close. And his mouth was brushing hers.

He managed, just barely, to keep the kiss light. Even so, he felt a rush of heat that left him shaken to the core.

As for Alex, her head swam, and for the space of several seconds, she tempted herself with the desire to melt into his arms. It was what she wanted. And what she'd been wanting for some time now. Instead she pushed free with a muttered, "So do I. It's called caffeine."

She crossed to the counter where she poured two cups of coffee. It was a source of pride that she managed to carry them to the table without spilling a drop, despite the fact that her hands were shaking.

Why did his simple touch do such strange things to her usually calm system?

She sat down, grateful that they had the table between them.

He bent to his breakfast. "What are you and Lem planning for today?"

"He thinks we ought to haul the snowmobiles out of storage and get them ready."

"He's still expecting that snowstorm?"

She nodded and nudged aside her cereal.

He glanced over. "What happened to your appetite?"

She shrugged and stepped away from the table. "I'm just not hungry. I'll eat later." As she pulled on her parka she looked over at him. "How're the hands?"

He couldn't hide his look of surprise as he glanced down at them. "Hey. How about that? The burning's gone."

"Any pain at all?"

He rubbed his hands together. "None."

"Well." She gave him a dimpled smile. "I'll expect your apology later, Mr. Malone."

"You can have it right now, Ms. Sullivan." He moved with such speed she had no time to react.

He caught her hand and lifted it to his lips. "I'm very grateful to you, my very own Florence Nightingale. And to show you my gratitude…" He dragged her against him and covered her mouth with his.

This time the kiss wasn't gentle. It was as hot and hungry as the look in those fierce dark eyes.

He'd wanted this. Needed it. And he'd held himself back too long. Now he simply indulged his fantasies as he took them both on a fast, dizzying ride.

She felt the flash, the heat, the need, and without giving a thought to what she was doing, responded to it. Twining her arms around his neck she pressed herself to the length of him and gave herself up to the pleasure. A pleasure that sent flames licking along her spine and nerves prickling at the back of her neck.

He lingered for a moment longer, savoring the sweet, clean taste of her and wanting more. Much more than a touch, a kiss.

When they finally drew apart, his gaze held hers. His voice was rough with need. ''You realize, Alex, sooner or later we're going to have to deal with this.''

''I know.'' She touched a hand on his chest and could feel the thundering of his heartbeat. Its erratic rhythm matched her own. She drew her hand back and took a step away.

He caught her hand, holding it a moment longer. ''If Lem wasn't out there waiting for you, we'd deal with it right now.''

She felt a tightening in her throat and knew that it wasn't fear. The fear of intimacy with him had long ago fled. Now it was something she craved as much as he did. This emotion clogging her throat had another name. Longing. She ached with it.

Reluctantly she turned and walked out the door. And though she didn't look back, she could feel him watching her. That knowledge excited her. In truth, everything about Grant Malone excited her.

There was no denying what was happening here. The change had been a gradual thing, and certainly not something they'd planned. But there it was. Both of them were hanging on to their control by a thread. And very soon now, that thread was bound to snap.

When it did, she wondered if she'd be able to catch hold of something solid and dependable. Or simply crash and burn.

"Think I'll fine-tune this engine a bit." Lem opened the hood of the snowmobile and began tinkering.

Beside him, Alex was pouring gasoline into the tank of a second machine.

When she heard the sound of the ax biting into wood, she glanced across the clearing, where Grant was chopping more logs.

Lem paused in his work to study her. She'd been flushed and breathless when she'd first left the kitchen. Now there was a look on her face he hadn't seen before. A tenderness that she usually reserved for the wounded wildlife. He'd swear he could almost see her heart there in her eyes. Then he followed her gaze to where Grant stood, arms lifted, muscles straining and was struck by how avidly she was watching every movement.

He hadn't been imagining it. She'd fallen. And from the look on her face, she'd fallen hard.

He hadn't intended to tell her what he'd learned about Grant. But now, seeing that look on her face, he figured she had a right to know.

He cleared his throat. "It took awhile. But I remember him now."

"Him?" Alex replaced the gas cap and glanced over at the old man.

"Grant Malone. Funny." He shook his head. "The name rang a bell the first time I heard it, but I just couldn't place it. And then he said something yesterday that got me thinking. Last night, just before I fell asleep, it all came back. Where I'd heard the name. Where I'd seen the face. He's that New York cop whose picture was in all the papers about six months ago. Caught in a shootout with a gang."

Alex gave a little gasp of surprise as she stared at him, eyes wide and unblinking. "The one who put himself in the line of fire for his partner? The one the newspapers were calling the Manhattan Hero?"

Lem nodded. "That's him. He took a couple of bullets before wiping out the entire gang. I remember reading later that his partner didn't survive. The doctors didn't expect Grant to make it either.

When he was released from the hospital the mayor gave him a fancy dinner and an award.''

Alex set down the gasoline can and slumped onto the seat of the snowmobile. "The Manhattan Hero. What do you think he's doing here?"

The old man shrugged. "You saw him when he arrived. Looked like one of those soldiers who saw too much combat.''

Alex thought about it a minute before nodding her head. "Post-traumatic stress. Battle fatigue." She sighed. "No wonder he sees danger behind every tree." She closed her eyes. "Oh, Lem. Can you imagine how angry he must have felt when I ordered him to lock up his gun?''

The old man laid a hand over hers. "Best thing you could have done. It's time he realizes this isn't New York City. Besides, that's your rule here at Snug Harbor Lodge. And he's a man who knows how to play by the rules.''

Play by the rules. Alex mulled those words while she watched Lem at work.

"I suppose I ought to let him know what we've learned about him.''

"It's your call. I'll leave that up to you, Alex.''

Seeing that she was deep in thought, Lem returned his attention to the snowmobile. Minutes later he twisted the key and the engine sprang to life, purring smoothly.

Alex lifted the gas can and began filling the second tank. Then, still lost in thought, she started toward the shed, carrying the half-empty can.

As she walked away, Lem thought about the gentle teasing he'd witnessed between Alex and Grant in the kitchen. Whatever private hell Grant Malone had been suffering when he'd first arrived, he seemed to be climbing out nicely, thanks to this simple place and one woman's gentleness.

The old man smiled to himself. Leave it to old Sully to deliver another wounded critter into his granddaughter's tender care. Nobody doctored them better.

He shook his head, wondering if Paddy Sullivan had thought about the consequences. He couldn't have known Alex might lose her heart in the process.

Lem glanced over at Grant, still swinging the ax with a burst of restless energy. He'd always wondered just what kind of man would finally win this special little female's heart. Now he knew. A tortured hero, who'd been willing to risk his life for another. It was the kind of loyalty Alex would admire and understand.

Though it wasn't his nature to meddle, Lem felt he owed it to her to see that she wasn't hurt. With a sigh he walked slowly toward Grant. He settled himself on a fallen log and casually pulled his pipe from his pocket, taking his time filling it with tobacco, holding a match to the bowl, then exhaling a wreath of smoke over his head.

Grant nodded toward the shed. "Does she ever slow down?"

"Not that I've noticed."

"She's amazing."

"Yep." Lem drew on his pipe, then watched the smoke curl up. "Got too much of a tender heart though."

"Why do you say that?"

"Sometimes it gets her hurt."

"In what way?"

The old man shrugged. "I remember once, a couple of years ago, she found a fox pup half-drowned in a pond, trapped in a rusted piece of fence wire."

"Did she manage to save him?"

Lem nodded. "Yeah. She freed him, and treated the festering wound to his leg. And the whole time, he snapped and snarled and struggled to break free."

"He must have been afraid. And hurting."

"That he was. When she finally released him, he thanked her by sinking his sharp little teeth into her finger. If you look close, you can still see the scar."

He tapped out the tobacco and crushed it beneath his boot. Then he stood and looked Grant in the eye. "I'd hate to see her bit by another wounded critter."

He tucked his pipe in his pocket and walked away.

Behind him, Grant watched in silence. And found himself wondering just what all that was about.

It was dark by the time the last chore was completed. Alex looked around the shed with a sense of satisfaction. Boat engines had been stored away and winterized. The snowmobiles were gassed and tuned and ready to roll. Behind the lodge, there was enough firewood to last through winter, and on into spring.

"Good thing we pushed ahead and didn't save anything for tomorrow," Lem remarked as he closed the shed door and latched it behind them.

"Why?"

He glanced toward the moon, shadowed by clouds. "See that haze? Snow's coming."

"Tonight?"

He nodded. "Could have ten inches or more by morning."

She smiled. "How's your knee?"

"A mite tender. It knows what's coming." He started toward his truck. "Guess I won't be seeing you for a couple of days. Plows might clear the main highways, but they won't bother with these back roads for a while. Need anything?"

She shook her head. "The lodge is in great shape, Lem, thanks to you. I'll be fine."

She stood on the porch and waved as he drove away. Then she turned and let herself inside.

In her room she took off her clothes and stepped into the shower. Half an hour later, dressed in woolen leggings and a knit tunic the color of ripe raspberries, she headed toward the kitchen.

As she passed through the great room she caught sight of a table positioned beside the window. It had been covered with a snowy linen cloth, and set with fine china, crystal and silver, gleaming in the light of flickering candles.

More candles glittered on a mirrored tray on the coffee table. A fresh log had been tossed on the fire, which added to the warmth and light.

Puzzled, Alex made her way to the kitchen. When she stepped inside, Grant turned from the stove. He was wearing fresh denims and a clean flannel shirt, with the sleeves rolled to the elbows.

"You're early."

"Early?" She arched a brow.

"I need another minute."

"What for?"

"The salmon. I'm poaching it in white wine. But that's all right. While we're waiting, I'll pour the champagne."

She watched in silence while he filled two flutes, then crossed the room and handed one to her.

She looked up into his face, and thought she detected a mysterious glint in his eyes. "What's the occasion?"

"Do we need a special reason to drink champagne?"

"I suppose not." She smiled. "But poached salmon?"

He gave a negligent shrug of his shoulders and touched his glass to hers. "We're reason enough, Alex."

She felt a shiver clear to her toes. It wasn't just the words, but the way he spoke them. It occurred to her that there was a whole lot more going on here than dinner. If she didn't know better, she'd believe he was planning a lovely seduction.

And she was about to spoil everything.

Oh, if only she hadn't learned the truth about him. But now that she knew, she couldn't pretend not to.

She sipped the champagne without even tasting it.

Grant hadn't moved. He continued to stand beside her, his body almost touching hers, looking at her in that intense way that always made her blood heat and her heart tremble.

Because she needed to step away she nodded

toward the serving cart, already laden with salads and rolls. "Would you like me to take that to the other room?"

"I'll take it." He set aside his champagne and removed the salmon from the oven. When it was covered, and placed on the cart, he nudged open the door and waited until Alex preceded him.

She paused in front of the fireplace. "Why did you set the table by the window?"

"Because you like the snow."

She looked up and could see a curtain of snowflakes dancing past the windowpane. "How did you know it would be snowing by dinnertime?"

"Lem's not the only one around who can predict the weather." He smiled. "I know how to dial the weather channel."

He waited for her answering smile. Instead she walked to the window and stared at the snow drifting past the window. But there was none of the expected joy in her eyes.

When she turned he held her chair and she took a seat while he served the salads. After only one bite she picked up her champagne and glanced at him across the table.

"Lem remembered where he'd seen you."

Grant's smile faded. He lowered his fork and stared at her in silence.

She sipped, then set aside her glass. "Your face was in all the papers. On TV. Lem didn't make the connection until you said something to him yesterday that started him thinking. You're the Manhattan Hero.''

He shoved away from the table and turned to stare out the window.

''It's the reason you came here.'' Not a question; a statement. For she realized now that he came here to Snug Harbor Lodge for a very different reason than most of the men. Not as a hunter, but as a seeker of healing solitude.

He gave a curt nod that made her feel like an intruder.

She fell silent, wishing there was something she could say or do to ease his pain. But as long as he continued to shut her out, she was helpless to know what he needed. And so she sat, the food he'd lovingly prepared growing cold, while he stood motionless, staring out at the darkness.

What was he seeing? she wondered. What demons stalked him day and night and caused him to suffer so?

When at last he started to speak, his voice was expressionless. ''The shrinks told me all this would fade in time.'' He made a sound that might have been a laugh or a sneer. ''I doubt there's enough time left in this world.''

''Are you afraid of dying? Is that what this is about?''

He shot her a startled glance. ''It's not dying I

fear. In fact, there have been times when I'd have welcomed death.'' He shook his head. ''No, Alex. It's not dying. It's living.'' He looked back out the window. ''You think you know who I am. Everybody thinks they know me now, from all the publicity. You said so yourself.'' His tone was filled with contempt. ''The Manhattan Hero.''

''You say that word as though it's an insult.''

''Not an insult. A fraud. That's me. The Manhattan Fraud.''

''Are you saying you didn't really put yourself in the line of fire to save your partner?''

He shrugged. ''That part is true. And why wouldn't I? He'd have done the same for me. Jason McClintock was not only my partner for eight years but also my best friend. I was the one who introduced him to my kid sister, Ellen. I was so happy when they fell in love and got married. After that, my best friend also became my brother-in-law.'' He gave a terse laugh. ''I used to boast that life just didn't get much better than that.''

Alex could hear the pain in his words. ''I hope you're not blaming yourself for Jason McClintock's death. The reports said that you did everything you could to save him. You even risked your own life for his.''

''Yeah. I'm sure that'll give my sister a lot of comfort in the years to come.'' He leaned his hands on the sill and pressed his forehead to the icy pane. "Just two days after we buried her husband, I stood by her while she gave premature birth to her baby. A boy. Jason's son. The son he'd been wanting from the first moment he knew they were going to have a baby. Poor Ellen. She looked so young and afraid. She became a wife, a mother and a widow all in the space of a single year. And now she's facing not just life, but new motherhood, alone."

"She won't be alone, Grant. She'll have her family and friends. She'll have you. You may not think you're a comfort to her, but you are. She'll never forget that you risked your own life to try to save her husband's. And her son will grow up knowing that, as well."

"The hero?" He spun around, and the fury in his eyes startled her. "Do you think I want my nephew growing up believing that myth?"

"Myth?"

"Yeah. The myth of the good guys and the bad guys. The noble cop who always triumphs over the villain. That's the kind of myth I grew up believing. Those are the stories my grandfather fed me from the time I was old enough to hear. Now I know better. And so will Jason's son one day. What will happen when he learns the truth?"

Alex kept her voice calm, even though her heart was pounding. "Just what is the truth, Grant?"

"The truth? You want the truth?" He turned

toward her and leaned his palms down on the table so that his eyes were level with hers. "Here's your truth, Alex. Not all bad guys look like monsters. Sometimes they aren't even old enough to shave. In my case the bad guy was just a kid. A sixteen-year-old kid."

The room was so silent, the only thing Alex could hear was the painful drumming of her heart-beat in her temples. She drew in a breath. "Did you know that when you shot him?"

He shook his head. "I couldn't see the shooter. He'd taken refuge behind a smashed car. He was part of a stolen car ring we'd been tracking. Jason had already taken a bullet to the chest. I knew it was bad. I just didn't know how bad. I pushed him aside and took the second bullet. Then I got a clear shot at the shooter, and I took it. And I killed a kid. I found out later his name was Wayne Kendrick. He was just sixteen years old."

Alex stood up, aware that her legs were trembling. In fact, her entire body was trembling. "I don't understand. Why are you beating yourself up about this? Wayne Kendrick may have been only sixteen, but he was old enough to fire a gun. It was your life or his."

His voice was low, angry. "You're right. You don't understand. Maybe I haven't made myself clear on this. I'm a crack shot. One of the best on the force. If I'd wanted, I could have taken Wayne

out without killing him. I could have put him out
of commission with a single shot in the leg, the
shoulder, the arm. But not our hero. I broke the
first rule of combat. I let myself get hot. Too hot
to make a rational judgment. He'd wounded my
partner. The bullet I'd taken was causing my body
to go numb. I was afraid I'd pass out before I could
end things and get Jason to a hospital. I didn't want
to take the time to do it right. So I took the easy
way out. I killed him with a single shot.'' His
shoulders slumped. ''And now a boy who had his
whole life ahead of him has run out of time.''

And there it was. At long last, she understood
the depth of his pain. This knowledge had appar-
ently been eating away at his soul until he'd become obsessed with it.

Alex took a deep breath, and thought about what
she could say that might ease his suffering. She
chose her words carefully.

''We all make choices in this life, Grant.
Choices that bring with them consequences. I'm
sure the doctors you've consulted have already
pointed out the obvious. This boy with the gun,
this sixteen-year-old Wayne Kendrick, had every
intention of using it on anyone who got in his way.
Your partner was only the first. If you hadn't
stopped him, there would have been others. Maybe
the next one would have been your sister. Or a
helpless child. Would you then fault the next cop

who came along and managed to stop him with a bullet?''

"Of course not. But that doesn't excuse the fact that his death is on my hands." He held them out, palms up, staring at them as if expecting to see bloodstains.

"You stopped him the only way you could. Maybe you didn't take the time to do it right. Maybe, if you could do it over, you'd take more time. But you had only a single second to make a life-and-death decision. None of this was your choice, Grant. The boy was the one who started the chain of events that ended with his death."

He heard the words. They were the same words he'd heard countless times before, when he'd made the rounds of doctors trained to help people in his profession deal with the trauma of death. But he heard only one word. Boy. It was a boy he'd killed; not a man. Not a monster.

"You say we all make choices. My problem is that I chose to be a police officer and carry a lethal weapon."

Alex hated the tears that sprang to her eyes. Hated the fact that her voice trembled with them. "You'd be surprised how many people in this world are grateful that you and others like you are willing to make that choice."

He lifted his gaze to look at her. Really look at her. And he could see that she had spoken from the heart. He saw the tears shimmering on her lashes. Heard the way her voice quivered with emotion.

''Even knowing that I took the life of that boy?''

She walked closer until she was standing in front of him. ''I suppose this grief, this horror over what you did, is what sets you apart, Grant. It's why the elected officials, and the men and women with whom you serve, wanted to honor you. They know that you aren't just an enforcer of laws. You feel a sense of responsibility for the people. All the people. Even those who make the wrong choices.''

She lifted her hands to his shoulders. Her voice was hushed. ''Maybe that's why I've come to care about you so deeply. Because you're still able, after all you've seen, after all you've been through, to grieve for the very boy who took your best friend's life.''

His dark gaze met and held hers. ''You…care about me?''

She nodded, too moved to speak.

He felt the tight band that had been around his heart all these long days and weeks begin to loosen its hold. Just a little. Enough to allow him to breathe.

''Even now, knowing all you do about me, you care about me?''

She lifted herself on tiptoe to press her lips to his. ''Let me show you how much I care, Grant.''

She was offering him everything he'd been hoping for. All these days and nights of wanting her. Now, finally, his for the taking. But suddenly he understood old Lem's warning. That sly old man had seen this coming.

The knowledge that he had the ability to hurt her was like a knife to the heart.

Instead of returning her kiss he took a step back. His voice was rough with impatience. "You don't want to be here with me right now."

She couldn't keep the shock and pain from slipping into her tone. "Why?"

He gave out a hiss of anger as he struggled to control the emotions simmering inside him. He had to do what he could to see that she didn't get hurt again. Otherwise, he'd be no better than that wounded fox.

His tone trembled with repressed fury. "I want to be alone now. I want you to leave me. Right now. This minute."

Chapter 10

The room had become so silent, Alex could actually hear her own breathing. Shallow and uneven as she looked at Grant. And her heartbeat, thundering in her ears.

Behind him the log crackled on the fire. But he said not a word. Only his eyes revealed his feelings. Eyes that smoldered.

"I don't understand. Wasn't all of this..." she swept a hand to indicate the table, the food, the candles "...intended as a seduction?"

"That was before." He looked away. It was easier than looking at her because when he did, he felt a pain around his heart that was worse than anything he'd suffered before. "Now I don't think

I'd be capable of sweet words and gentle seduction. There's too much darkness in me. I'm afraid if I touch you now, I'll hurt you. Right this minute, all I want to do is ravish you.''

"I've never been…ravished.'' She laughed lightly as she touched a hand to his chest and felt the way his heart suddenly jolted. "I think I might like it.''

He absorbed a series of tremors that had his nerves scrambling and his mind screaming with need. He thought about crushing her in his arms. Instead he fisted his hands at his sides. ''This isn't a game, Alex. There's a part of me you don't know. A part of me I don't want you to know. Unless you leave right now, I'm going to do things to you you've never even thought about.''

She saw the way his muscles bunched and tensed as he clenched and unclenched his fists at his sides. It was the most amazing thing to watch the flames leap into his eyes even while he fought for control. Watching the battle he was waging with himself excited her. Aroused her even more.

"I think I know you better than you know yourself.''

"Do you?'' His eyes narrowed. "You think I'm some sort of hero. But I'm not, Alex. I'm just a man. Not a very nice one at the moment. I'd want to be gentle, but I wouldn't be able to control myself. I've waited too long. Wanted you too long.''

His tone lowered with passion. "Would it shock you to know that right now I want to tear your clothes off you? I want to touch you, taste you. Everywhere."

At the intensity of his words she shivered.

He saw fear leap into her eyes before she blinked. But to her credit, she didn't back away. Instead, she ran a tongue over her dry lips and brought one hand to his cheek.

She felt a muscle begin to work in his jaw. "I think I'm a little afraid."

"You should be."

"Not of you. Of myself. Of how I'll react if I stay."

"Then turn and run, Alex. And never look back."

She brushed her thumb over his mouth and heard his little intake of breath. "It's too late for that. I've never run from anything in my life. And I'm not about to start now." She drew herself close, until their bodies were touching. Then she lifted her head and stared into his eyes. "I'm staying, Grant. No matter what."

For the space of a heartbeat he waited, unable to believe what he'd just heard. Then, as the truth of her words sank in, his arms came around her, pressing her to the length of him while his mouth savaged hers. There would be time later for gentleness. Time to taste, to savor. For now, all he

could do was take and take, like a man too-long
starved.

Stunned, she made a sound in her throat that
might have been a sob or a cry. It was swallowed
by another kiss that had her world tilting, her mind
wiped clean of every thought except one. She
never wanted him to stop.

Her arms encircled his neck and she offered her
mouth willingly. But instead of kissing her he
drove her back against the wall and lifted her until
she was wrapped around him. Her head swam as
she realized this was exactly as he'd warned her.
No gentle seduction. Nor would he allow some
sweet surrender. Instead, what he wanted, what he
demanded of her, was complete participation.

His lips covered her savagely. And all the while,
his hands moved down her back, lighting fires
wherever they touched.

His hands were almost bruising as they cupped
her hips. "I can't make you any promises."

"I'm not asking for any."

She wouldn't, he thought. She was too open, too
generous.

Starving, he lowered his mouth to hers. There
was such hunger in him. Such need. But the more
he took, the more she offered, until he groaned and
filled himself with the taste of her.

He knew that without the press of the wall behind her they would already be on the floor, where

he feared he would take her like a savage. But he couldn't seem to stop. He wanted more. He wanted all.

"Maybe we should…slow things down." She whispered the words against his mouth, which only managed to drive him closer to the edge.

In one smooth motion he pulled the tunic over her head and tossed it aside. Underneath she wore silk. He hadn't expected to discover that this simple woman, who dressed in denims and boots, would pamper herself with such luxury. It was surprising. And deeply erotic.

He slipped one silken strap from her shoulder to expose the soft swell of her breast. Then he bent his lips to the spot. She was helpless to do more than sigh as his lips and fingertips moved over her, arousing her to a fever pitch.

He hated even this tiny barrier between them, and with one tug easily disposed of the piece of silk. Now he could see her skin, as cool and pale as cream. With an animal sound low in his throat he took one breast into his mouth.

The shock of it swept through her with all the force of an icy blade, piercing her to the very core. With each tug of that warm, clever mouth, she took another knife thrust, until she was nearly overcome with sensations.

He moved from one breast to the other, driving both Alex and himself to the edge of madness.

How had she lived so long without this? she wondered, as he slipped a finger under the waistband of her leggings and tugged them from her. They drifted to the floor as he found her, hot and moist, and brought her to the first sudden, shocking peak.

She was so stunned her knees buckled, and she would have fallen if not for his hands holding her firmly.

"Grant." His name was torn from her lips.

Frantic to touch him as he was touching her, she unbuttoned his shirt and skimmed it aside to run her hands over his back. She thrilled to the feel of firm flesh, and beneath it, the layers of muscle.

"Say that again." His eyes, steady on hers, burned with a strange light.

"What?" She had to struggle to concentrate. The feel of that wonderful body against hers had her mind spinning out of control.

"My name. Say it, Alex."

"Grant." She smiled then, and brushed her lips across his jaw. "Grant. Grant. Oh, hold on to me."

"Don't worry." He ran nibbling kisses across her cheek and jaw, and lower still to her throat until she trembled in his arms. "I'm not letting go."

He couldn't get enough of her. Of those warm, perfect lips. Of those small, firm breasts. Of all that hot, steamy flesh that seemed to melt in his hands.

She smelled of soap and shampoo, and some light fragrance that reminded him of evergreen. The thought of devouring her right here on the floor, inch by glorious inch, had the blood throbbing in his loins.

She was sighing, then sobbing, as he dropped to his knees before her and took her on a wild, dizzying climb.

"Grant." His name came out on a shudder as she felt herself tremble, then soar to new heights.

She was wonderful to watch. It was as though she'd never experienced any of this before. She made him feel powerful. She made him feel new. She made him feel whole.

He brought his mouth back up her body to claim her lips once more.

She reached trembling hands to the fasteners at his waist, frantic to see him. To touch him. She wanted no more barriers between them.

When her fingers fumbled he helped her until he'd managed to kick aside the last of his clothes. Then he dragged her into his arms and lowered his mouth to hers.

"Think we can make it to a bed?"

She laughed, that wonderful velvet sound that always seemed to wrap itself around him. "You want a bed, do you? All right. We can try."

He lifted her into his arms and started out of the great room. But before he'd taken half a dozen steps, he had to pause to cover her mouth with his. One greedy kiss led to another, and they staggered before he found the strength to tear his mouth from hers and attempt a few more steps.

They were laughing when they made it to his room. It was closer than hers by a few steps. At the moment every step seemed like a mile.

He kicked open the door, then strode across the room to lower her to the bed before he joined her.

"I didn't think we'd make it." She rolled over him and sent his pulse into overdrive when she began running hot, wet kisses across his chest, then lower, to the flat planes of his stomach.

"You're killing me." Half-mad with desire, he rolled them both over and trailed his mouth down the length of her body and back.

The world beyond had slipped away. Outside a snowstorm raged and howled, but it was nothing compared to the storm of passion raging between them. All they knew were the wild, frantic touches, the heady taste, the dark, musky scent of desire. It clogged their throat. Blurred their vision. Clouded their minds. And drove them closer and closer to the brink of insanity.

And still there was no relief.

Grant felt himself slipping toward the edge of madness and tried to slow down. But he knew it was futile. They were both caught up in a tide of passion that was sweeping them along with all the force of a blizzard.

Still, he had to try. He kissed her long and slow and deep, and allowed the taste of her to seep into him. "So clean. You taste as fresh as new snow."

"And you taste...dangerous." She lifted a hand to his face, to trace a finger over the curve of his brow. "That first night, when you dragged me onto this bed, I thought you were a hit man."

"Did you?" That brought a laugh from deep in his throat. "The first time I heard your name, Alexandra, I thought it the most beautiful sound in the world."

"You did?" She smiled.

He nodded. "And I wanted this. Only this." Calling on all his control, he forced himself to be gentle as he ran soft, nibbling kisses over her face, and down the long, smooth column of her throat.

"And I wanted this." She drew his face to hers until their mouths met for a slow, lingering kiss.

"Alexandra." He took the time to study the way she looked, her skin flushed from his kisses, her eyes heavy-lidded with passion.

"I never liked my name before. I suppose that's why I insisted on being called Alex."

"Then I may have to call you Alexandra from now on. Because the name is as beautiful as you."

His hands tangled in her hair while his mouth explored her neck, her throat, her shoulder. But when his lips moved lower she sighed out a breath of pleasure.

He loved the way she looked, her body soft and pliant, her eyes glazed with pleasure. But as the pleasure grew and became more intense, so did the heat, the need. As his hands moved over her she began to writhe and moan beneath him.

"I've wanted you for such a long time." He whispered the words against her mouth, then inside her mouth, as he devoured.

"I've wanted you, too."

Her admission only fueled his hunger. With lips and teeth and tongue he had them both spinning out of control.

Against her mouth his voice was harsh with frustration. "If I don't take you soon, I'm going to explode."

She saw a look in his eyes that was dark and dangerous, and as close to violence as she'd ever seen. But instead of fear, she felt a heightened sense of excitement.

"Hurry, then. I want you, too. Now."

She'd never known such greed. But the desire for more pleasure prodded her to wrap herself around him, to take them both higher. She wanted to take and give until they were both sated.

She arched her hips in welcome as he drove himself into her. And though she'd thought it impossible to want more, she did. As she began to move with him, to climb with him, she knew she wanted it all.

"Alexandra." Her name was torn from his lips. "My sweet, tenderhearted, beautiful Alexandra."

He kept his eyes steady on hers as he took her up, then over. This was how he'd wanted to see her. Mad with desire. All her defenses gone. And as wildly out of control as he felt at this moment.

His, he thought. For now, for this moment, this wonderful, beautiful treasure was all his.

Then his mind was wiped clean of thought as he felt her shudder and collapse against him. At his own sudden, violent climax, he cried out her name again. Or thought he did as he held her close and felt his body shattering into millions of bright, shiny pieces, before drifting back to earth.

Chapter 11

Grant lay perfectly still, amazed that he was still breathing. He'd thought for a moment that he'd died. He'd felt himself splintering, then falling to earth like a snowflake. He closed his eyes, unwilling to break the spell.

Alex wasn't a woman who wept easily. But as they lay, still joined, bodies slick with sheen, she found herself on the verge of tears. She blinked and dragged in a steadying breath.

Feeling it, he levered himself on his hands to look down at her. When he caught the glint of a tear on her lashes, he felt his heart stop.

"What's this?" With a muttered oath he touched a finger to the moisture. "I can't believe

I could be so rough. Oh, baby, I'm sorry. I didn't mean…''

She reached up to press a finger to his lips. Her eyes were still shiny, but her lips curved into a smile. ''I don't know what's come over me. I never cry. But…'' she drew his face down and touched her lips to his ''…that was just so incredible.''

His heart skipped a beat. ''Then you're not sorry?''

''Sorry?'' She kissed him again, and gave a ripple of laughter. ''The only thing I'm sorry about is that we waited so long.''

''Is that all?'' He threw back his head and laughed, and felt his heart begin to beat again. Then he rolled aside and drew her into his arms, and marveled at the way she seemed to fit so perfectly against him. ''If you're really sorry, we could always go for seconds.''

''You're a greedy man, Mr. Malone.''

''Yeah. But I think there's a little greed in you, too, Ms. Sullivan.'' He brushed his mouth over hers and felt the quick rush of heat. How was it possible that he could want her again so soon?

He shifted his focus to the window. ''Did you see what's going on out there while we were… otherwise engaged?''

She turned. ''Oh, Grant. Isn't it beautiful?''

''Yeah. As long as we're on the inside looking out.''

"That's just it. We're in here, all snug and warm, and Mother Nature is out there decorating our world for us."

He shook his head in wonder. "It doesn't take much to make you happy, does it?"

"Not much. A snowfall. A cozy fire. A man who can kiss me until my head spins."

He leaned close and brushed his mouth over hers. "Happy to oblige, ma'am." After a moment he slid from the bed. "I'll just add a log to that fire and be right back for more of that."

As he turned she caught sight of the ridge of scars along his back and thought about all the pain he'd suffered. Not just the physical pain, which must have been nearly overpowering, but the mental anguish as well.

"Oh, Grant." When he returned to bed she touched a hand to the spot. "This must have been so horrible."

The minute the words had been spoken, she regretted them. But he managed a grim smile.

"It goes with the job. You either accept that, or you walk."

"Is that why you're here? You walked?"

He shook his head. "I'm here to sort out a few things. Then I'll decide if I stay or walk."

She tentatively touched a hand to the ridge of scars. "Is there any lingering pain?"

He shrugged. "Some. But I can live with it."

She pressed her lips to the spot. "I wish there was something I could do."

He drew her close and nuzzled her temple, feeling the heat begin to grow again, and with it, the hunger. "You already have, Alex. My beautiful, wonderful Alexandra. Just by being here in my arms. In my bed." He felt a wave of sudden tenderness. "Now about that greed we both seem to harbor, Ms. Sullivan..."

He ran his hands along her sides and his thumbs found her breasts. At his mere touch they seemed to swell against his palms. She had a sudden, urgent need to pleasure him as he had pleasured her. To feed the hunger that she could see in his eyes. To fill the need that she could taste in every kiss. She wanted, she realized, to comfort him. To make him forget, for at least a little while, all the things he had endured. But all she could give him was this. Slow, passionate kisses. And a touch that was soothing, even while it aroused.

Her reaction to his touch had his head spinning. "If I'd known how easy you were, I'd have tried this a long time ago."

"I may be easy, but there will be a price to pay."

He paused.

"You promised to feed me. And I intend to hold you to that."

"You're a hard woman, Alexandra Sullivan."

Her eyes glinted with mischief as she straddled him, causing him to suck in his breath. "Hmm. And amazingly, you're a hard man. Again."

"Exactly. Which is why we're a perfect match." While he kissed her long and slow and deep, his hands began weaving their magic.

As he lost himself in her he felt a welling of such emotion for this woman, who had heard the plea of his tormented soul and had answered it. She'd managed, with her simple generous nature, to reach him in a way that none of the experts had been able to do.

And as he poured out all his feelings in a torrent of lovemaking, he felt the long-denied healing begin at last.

"Mmm." Sitting up in bed Alex sampled the salmon from the plate Grant handed her.

"It would have tasted better a couple of hours ago." Barefoot, wearing only jeans unsnapped at the waist, he tossed another log on the fire, then hurried over to settle down beside her.

He studied the way she looked, her hair tumbled around a face that glowed in the light of the fire. She had pulled on one of his flannel shirts for warmth. Unbuttoned, it skimmed her breasts, barely covering her nakedness. She was so beautiful she took his breath away. He still couldn't believe she was here with him.

"I've been meaning to tell you. That looks a heck of a lot better on you than it does on me."

"Thanks. That's because I'm prettier."

"You'll get no argument from me."

"Well, I could say you're pretty, too. For a man."

"Thanks, I think." He grinned. "How's the salmon?"

"It's wonderful." She held the fork to his mouth and he took a bite, then nodded his approval before reaching for the bottle of champagne.

"Not bad, considering it had to be nuked. Better see that you eat plenty of it." He filled two flutes and handed one to her.

"Why?"

He shot her a dangerous grin. "Because you may want to fortify yourself. If the past couple of hours are any indication, I'd say we're both going to need all the strength we can get."

"Don't worry about me, Mr. Malone. If I can hike clear around the lake and up into those hills, I think I can keep up with you."

He caught her chin and brushed his lips over hers. "No doubt about that, Ms. Sullivan." He saw the slight flush that colored her cheeks and knew that she'd felt the heat as surely as he. "Unless I decide to try a new tactic."

"And what would that be?"

"This." He took the flute from her hands and

placed it beside his on the night table. Then he caught her foot and tugged until she was lying flat. Without warning he began nibbling on her toes, which sent her into spasms of laughter.

"Stop! Oh, Grant. Stop. Please."

"Let's see if you can keep up with me now, Nature Girl. We're not just hiking forests and mountains. This is something much more challenging."

He began running kisses across the arch of her foot, her ankle, the back of her knee. As he brought his mouth higher, he paused to glance at her. The laughter had died, replaced with a look of astonishment, and then of pleasure.

"Still want me to stop?"

She was beyond words as he brought her to a sudden, shocking crest. And then, as he took them both on a slow, erotic journey, all she could do was hold on for the ride of a lifetime.

"What made you decide to be a cop?"

They were sitting in bed, sipping mugs of coffee, with the first faint hint of dawn light spilling into the room. A fire blazed on the hearth, chasing away the chill.

"I told you about my grandfather, Mickey. I grew up listening to his stories of heroes and villains, and good always winning over evil." While he talked, Grant played with the ends of her hair.

It felt so good to be able to touch her, whenever, wherever he pleased. "I was a good student, and both my parents thought I'd follow them into the field of teaching. My father is a professor of mathematics at New York University, and my mother teaches high school English. My sister, Ellen, taught first grade until she took a maternity leave. The family was pretty upset for a while when I announced that I wanted to go into law enforcement. But eventually they came around and understood that I loved what I was doing." His voice lowered. "Until now. Now I don't know what my future holds. I've dealt with the psychologists and the medical profession, and I've been advised to take as much time as I need to heal and decide where I want to go from here."

"I bet your grandfather could give you some advice. Have you talked to him about this?"

He nodded. "A little. As much as I was able. He understands, even though he admits he never had to deal with anything quite like this." Grant leaned back, amazed at how easy and natural it seemed to talk with Alex about this. "But I think he feels confused about why I'd ever consider leaving law enforcement. He was so proud that I'd joined the academy. And so proud the day I earned my badge."

"That's wonderful."

"Yeah." He drew her close and brushed his mouth over hers. "So are you."

"Careful." She steadied her cup. "I wouldn't want to spill this."

"Neither would I." He took the mug from her hand and set it beside his on the night table, then gave her one of those heart-stopping smiles. "Now I'll give you a proper kiss."

"You really shouldn't." As they came together she muttered, "You know what this always leads to."

"Yeah. That's what I'm counting on."

With a sigh she sank into his embrace. And allowed him to take her on a fast, heart-stopping journey of delight.

Thin morning light seeped into the room, along with the eerie white light that always signaled a snowfall.

Alex awoke on a sigh of contentment and sat up, sweeping the tangles back from her face before glancing at the man beside her. She found herself studying that beautiful sculpted body, like a warrior of old, honed for battle. Ever so gently she traced the remnants of the bullet wounds he bore, several of which might have sent a lesser man to his grave. But they were nothing compared with the wounds to his heart and soul. She prayed the day would soon come when they would be nothing more than the shadows of scars. And the pain of them would dim to a distant memory.

"So solemn." He lifted a finger to the little frown line between her brows. "Have I made you so unhappy?"

She shook her head, sending that rich cloud of hair dancing around her face. "I can't remember when I've ever felt better or more alive."

"Then why the frown? What're you thinking?"

"That we've been in this bed for hours. If we keep this up, we're going to grow lazy."

"Oh. I see. It's strenuous activity you're looking for, is it?"

"Mm-hmm." As she started to slide from the bed his hand closed around her wrist, holding her still.

She turned and shot him a look.

He grinned. "Come here, woman. I have the perfect activity in mind to get the blood pumping and the muscles stretching."

"I'll just bet you do." But she allowed herself to be dragged into his arms without protest.

And then, as he brought his mouth to her throat and began to nibble his way lower, she found herself purring. "I like the way you get your exercise, Sergeant Malone."

"It's Captain Malone. And I thought you might." He moved over her body until she hummed with need. "I think you'll like this, too."

As he brought his mouth lower, the sound in her throat changed from a purr to a growl.

"And this. And…"

"Grant…"

"Shh. Not a sound. We'll just get in a little healthy exercise."

And then there was no need for words as they took each other on another slow, delicious journey.

Chapter 12

"Where are you going?" Feeling the mattress shift as Grant moved away, Alex automatically reached for him.

He leaned over to kiss the tip of her nose. "Not far. Thought I'd toss another log on the fire. I just realized it's cold in here."

Alex sat up as the realization dawned. "The heat. I'll bet it's gone out." She slid out of bed and began hastily pulling on his flannel shirt.

"Why would the heat go out?"

"That's why." She pointed to the window. "All that heavy snow probably knocked out some power lines." She hurried from the room.

Minutes later she returned to find him standing across the room, staring out the window.

He turned as she entered. "We must have had a foot or more of snow last night. It's as high as the woodpile in places." He shook his head. "If we ever had this much snow in New York City, we'd have to shut it down." He paused, listening. "What's that sound?"

"Hmm?" She walked up beside him to enjoy the view, her eyes as wide as a child's. "Oh, the generator. The power's out."

"Can't you call someone?"

She laughed. "Don't worry. It happens a lot up here. We're used to it. That's why we have a backup generator. I just switch it on and we have just about as many comforts as when the power is on. We'll have to conserve hot water, and we'll use more wood in the fireplace. Other than that, there's very little inconvenience until the line crews can get through the snow."

"Conserve hot water, you say?" He grinned. "I'm all for that. From now on, we'll just shower together. I've been wanting to put that huge shower to some use."

She gave a mock-pained expression. "I can see that you're feeling really inconvenienced by all this."

He chuckled and gathered her close. "It's a tough life out here in the wilderness. But I'm learning to survive." He caught her hand and started toward the shower. "Come on, Nature Girl. I'll let you scrub my back."

Wearing woolen leggings and a heavy turtleneck, Alex made her way to the kitchen, breathing in the rich fragrance of sausage and onion and potatoes on the grill. "How wonderful. I see you fixed breakfast."

"I was in need of a real he-man breakfast. After all, thanks to you, I exerted a lot of energy through the night."

"Hmm." She studied the grill, then turned toward the toaster. "Is that cinnamon toast I smell?"

Grant nodded. "And scrambled eggs."

She opened the refrigerator and poured juice. "I was thinking more along the lines of cold cereal."

"That's for wimps. This morning we're going to eat."

"Maybe you're right." She danced across the room in a burst of excitement to peer once more out the window. "With all that snow to play in, you'll need to be fortified."

"Play?" He nibbled a piece of toast while he served their plates. "You really want to play in the snow?"

"Isn't that why nature gave it to us?" She was already sipping her juice and fairly twitching with excitement. But when she bit into the first sausage, she shot him a look. "You've been holding out on

me. You really do know how to cook all kinds of
different things. This is wonderful.''

"Oh, it's nothing, ma'am. But you really ought
to taste my beef tenderloin marinated in my own
concoction of red wine and spices. I don't like to
brag, but there are master chefs who would pay a
fortune for the recipe.''

She laughed. "It just so happens that I have a
lovely tenderloin in the freezer that I've been saving for a special occasion. Would you like me to
thaw it for dinner?''

"It would be my pleasure. But if I'm going to
do the cooking, you have to promise to do the
cleanup.''

"Promise.'' She pushed away from the table and
returned with a parcel in butcher's wrap. "Do with
this what you wish, Chef Malone.''

He wiggled his brows and gave a dangerous
grin. "Careful. Women have been known to offer
to become my slaves after the first taste of Tenderloin Malone.''

"Uh-huh.'' She couldn't resist laughing as she
finished her breakfast. "We'll see about that slave
bit. For now, let's hurry. I can't wait to get out in
all that snow.''

Minutes later she shoved away from the table
and began slipping into her parka and boots.

Grant took one last sip of coffee, then reached
for his parka hanging by the back door. As she

twisted a scarf around his neck he caught her by the shoulders and nuzzled her temple. "Sure you wouldn't rather have fun indoors? I've still got a few things I'd like to show you."

"I'll just bet you do." She laughed and pushed away. "But right now, you're going to enjoy some real fun in the outdoors."

"Okay." He grabbed up a pair of gloves and trailed her out the door. "But I'll bet the fun I had planned is better than yours."

"You can show me yours later."

That brought a huge grin to his face. "You can count on it."

Catching the double meaning, she burst into laughter as she led the way outside, where the porch was piled knee-deep with snow. They trudged through it to the shed, where Alex pointed to a snowblower. "We can use this to make a path to the porch."

"This is your idea of fun?"

"First we work," she said with a laugh. "Then we play. Besides, this kind of work really is play."

"So you say. But this sounds suspiciously like the things my mother used to tell me when I was a kid and she wanted to get the chores done." In a falsetto he intoned, "Come on, Grant honey. Clean your room and mow the lawn. Take out the garbage, and sweep out the garage, and then you can have some of my home-baked chocolate chip cookies. As long as you help me bake them.''

Alex was laughing so hard she could hardly speak. Finally, she found her voice. ''Okay. You're wise to me. So let's get that path to the porch, and then we can play.''

''Why don't I believe you?'' Though he grumbled, he started the snowblower and began clearing a path through the mounds of snow.

While Grant finished that chore, Alex shoveled the porch and swept the snow from the woodpiles. Together they hauled logs indoors, setting enough beside each fireplace to last them for several days.

''Now I suppose you'll want me to plow the driveway,'' Grant teased.

''It wouldn't do us any good. With all this snow, we're not going anywhere.''

''You mean we're socked in here? No one from the outside world can disturb us?''

''That's right.'' She touched a hand to his cheek. ''Just you and me, alone together.''

He caught her hand and pressed a kiss to the palm. ''I like the sound of that.''

''I'll just bet you do. Come on. Our chores are done.''

''Really?''

She nodded. Catching his hand she led him outside. ''Time to play.''

As she started to scoop up snow in her mittens

he merely looked at her as though she'd lost her mind. Then, when it dawned on him that she was making a snowman, he joined in, rolling a second huge ball which he placed on top of hers. They added a third, and even a fourth, until he was as tall as a real man.

"He needs eyes," Alex called, rummaging through the snow until she found a couple of stones.

"And a hat." Grant went inside and returned with a bright red stocking cap and a long woolen scarf which he twisted around and tied in a loop.

They stood back admiring their handiwork.

"He needs something." Alex crossed her arms over her chest, regarding the snowman.

"A snow-woman," Grant muttered.

"Exactly. How did you know?"

"Because he looks lonely."

They bent to their work, rolling more giant snowballs and placing them to one side of the snowman. While Grant hunted a few branches from evergreens and leaves from nearby trees for hair, Alex hurried indoors and returned with a brightly colored shawl, which she securely knotted so that it wouldn't blow away.

"That's better." Grant added more snow between the two figures, then used a stick to fashion fingers, which appeared to be linked.

He stepped back, then caught Alex by the hand

and linked his fingers with hers. "Yeah. Much better." He regarded them carefully, then turned to her with a grin. "She's not bad for a snow-woman. I wonder if she can cook."

"You thinking of replacing me?"

"It's a possibility."

She bent and rolled a snowball, then tossed it, hitting him squarely on the cheek. "You'd better watch what you're thinking, Captain Malone. I won't tolerate any two-timing."

"Now you've done it." He wiped the snow from his face with his hand, then bent to roll a snowball of his own. "You want to do battle, do you?"

Alex ducked, and the snowball landed harmlessly beside her. But his second one didn't miss. Nor the third, which splattered against her neck, then began dripping inside the collar of her parka.

"Now you've done it." Ducking behind a tree for cover she began frantically scooping up snowballs and tossing them.

Grant charged, taking several hits to the face and neck before pinning her arms to her sides. Then, still holding her firmly, he dragged her to the ground and grabbed a handful of snow.

"Now as I see it, you have two choices, Ms. Sullivan. You can admit defeat and declare me the winner, or you're going to have one very cold, very wet face. Which would be a pity, since it's such a pretty face.''

"That's what they all say.'' She writhed and wriggled beneath him, and found that despite her strength, she couldn't dislodge him. "Grant, you wouldn't dare.''

"You're talking to a man who has never been able to resist a dare.'' He lowered his hand until the snow was inches from her face. "Which will it be?''

She lifted her chin defiantly. "It's simply not in my nature to admit defeat. Even in the face of overwhelming odds. So...''

She watched as he brought the snow closer. But instead of smearing it over her face, he suddenly tangled his fingers in her hair and covered her mouth in a searing kiss.

Alex could taste the heat, the fire, the passion, all wrapped up in a single kiss. She marveled that even now, after a night of lovemaking, there could be so much need inside him. A hunger that spoke to a similar hunger, an aching loneliness, deep inside her.

"I'm willing to call it a draw,'' he whispered against her lips.

"Only because you realize I was about to trounce you.''

"Lady, you had me beat the minute I laid eyes on you. Right now, I'd give in to anything you asked for, as long as you let me kiss you like this again.''

She laughed, but the laugh soon became a sigh as he brought his mouth to hers for another drugging kiss.

When she managed to catch her breath she rolled aside and caught his hand, helping him to his feet. ''Come on.''

His eyes lit with hope. ''Where are we going? Inside to finish this?''

''Not a chance. We're going ice skating. I can see that you have a lot of restless energy that needs to be put to good use.''

''I know a perfect way to put it to use.''

''I'm wise to you, Malone. Come on.'' She caught his hand and led him to the shed, where there were more than a dozen pair of ice skates in various sizes hanging along one wall.

He studied the skates until he located his size. ''You're prepared for anything, aren't you?''

''This is a lodge that caters to its guests' whims. We've been known to get hit with snowstorms in the middle of September. If our guests can't hunt or fish, they can always go hiking or skating.''

She tossed him a snow shovel. ''Before we can skate, we'll have to clear away the snow.''

''Uh-huh. Another chore disguised as fun.''

Alex merely laughed.

They carried their skates and shovels to the

pond. Using a fallen log for a bench, they laced their skates, then took to the ice and began to shovel the snow until they'd uncovered enough space for a rink. Tossing aside the shovels they began to make slow, lazy circles around the ice.

Alex watched as Grant smoothly cut across the rink. "This isn't your first time on skates."

"I used to play hockey."

"Really? So did I. I was the first girl allowed to play with our men's team in college."

He paused beside her. "Why am I not surprised by that?"

She shook her head. "If it had to do with the outdoors, I was just naturally attracted. I was willing to let my sisters be cheerleaders. I wanted to be in the thick of the action."

Grant caught her hand. "Come on. Let's see if we can do a couple of turns together."

They began to move around the perimeter, and found to their delight that they were able to skate in perfect harmony. After a couple of minutes Grant dropped an arm around her shoulder and drew her close. She leaned into him and they glided across the ice.

"You're good, Ms. Sullivan."

"You're not bad yourself, Captain Malone."

"Want to try for the Olympics?"

"We're not that good." She laughed. "But it's

fun finding someone who doesn't have two left feet.''

"Yeah. I was just thinking the same thing.''

They slowed their pace until they were standing in the middle of the ice, looking into each other's laughing eyes. It seemed the most natural thing in the world to come together, arms around each other, mouths mating.

Suddenly there was no cold. Only heat. And the feeling that they were the only two people in this vast universe.

Grant drew a little away and caught her hand. "Come on. Time we got in out of the cold. If we stay out here any longer, we may both be as frozen as our snowpeople.''

They took off their skates and slipped into their boots before picking up the shovels and heading for the shed.

At the door of the lodge they kicked snow off their boots before stepping inside. As they hung their parkas and set their hats, gloves and scarves on a drying rack, Alex was achingly aware of Grant beside her. As soon as she'd shed her outerwear, he dragged her close for another kiss.

He lingered over her lips, then buried his face in her hair and crushed her against him. "If you want me to keep my promise to feed you, you'd better let me love you first. Otherwise, I'm afraid I might devour you along with that tenderloin.''

She gave a shaky laugh. ''I wouldn't want to spoil such a promising dinner. Besides, I don't think I can wait either.''

Like two eager children they caught hands and raced to the bedroom.

''That was amazing.'' Alex leaned back into the softness of the sofa and drained her wine.

''The meal?'' He leaned over to refill her glass. ''Or what came before?''

''Are you fishing for compliments?''

''Of course.'' He shot her a dangerous smile. ''A man likes to know that he's superior in…all things.''

''I was talking about the meal. I don't know when I've tasted tenderloin that perfect.''

''And how about the…appetizer?''

She glanced sideways and caught the smug look on his face. ''It was fair.''

''Only fair?''

She shrugged. ''What it lacked in flavor was more than made up for by the chef's…enthusiasm.''

''You want flavor?'' He reached over and took the glass from her hand.

Before she realized what he intended he began running nibbling kisses from her cheek to her jaw to her throat. She sighed with pure pleasure. But just as she began to relax, he reached for the but-

tons of her blouse. With his eyes steady on hers
he slid it from her shoulders and parted the silk he
knew he'd find beneath. With that last barrier removed, he began to taste, to feast, until she could
feel her mind begin to cloud and her bones dis-
solve.

"Grant. The dishes..."

"Will still be here later."

"But I..." Her protest died in her throat as he
proceeded to slowly drive her mad.

Later, as they sat by the fire and finished the last
of their wine, Alex glanced at the curtain of snow
falling past the window.

"It's snowing again."

Grant saw the way her eyes went all soft and
dreamy and couldn't help smiling. "Does that
mean you'll want to play again tomorrow?"

"And what if I do?"

He lifted her hand to his mouth and pressed a
kiss there. "Hey. I'm not complaining. I like the
way you play. And I really like the way you warm
up afterward. Speaking of which..." He stood and
tugged on her hand, bringing her to her feet. "Let's
watch the snow from my bedroom window."

"You're a glutton."

"Not at all. I'm just looking out for your comfort." He led the way down the hall and drew her
into his arms as they stepped into his bedroom.

''Now we can watch the snow and keep each other warm at the same time.''

It was, she realized, just about the best way of all to spend a long winter's night.

Chapter 13

Alex hauled down snowshoes hanging on hooks along one wall and tossed a pair to Grant.

He neatly caught them. "We're going hiking?"

"That's right. To the very top of the hill."

They'd spent the morning removing the additional six inches of snow that had fallen overnight. Now, with a clear path from the shed to the lodge, and the porch and woodpile neatly swept, they were ready to play.

He reached up and removed a toboggan from a shelf. "If we're hiking up, I intend to take the easy way back down."

"That little toy could get pretty heavy by the time we're halfway up the hill."

He laughed. "Yeah. But think how handy it'll be when we're ready to come down."

She latched the door behind them, then fastened her snowshoes and caught hold of the toboggan rope. Grant did the same, and they began walking toward the distant slope.

As they rounded the lake Alex pointed. "Isn't that the prettiest picture you've ever seen?"

Grant paused to study it. Fresh snow had already completely obliterated yesterday's rink. The limbs of the trees lining the shore were bent to the ground, heavy with snow. A few ducks circled overhead, then left to find open water. The scene was almost too perfect to be believed.

Alex's voice was hushed with a sort of reverence. "Do you know what I like best?"

Grant shook his head.

"There are no prints except ours."

He turned to study the two sets of prints left by their snowshoes and the toboggan that skimmed across the snow, leaving little more than a wide, rough swath.

"It's like having a clean slate." She gave a last look over the vast white countryside, then turned away to continue the upward trek.

As he moved along beside her, Grant found himself loving the image of a clean slate. That's how being here with Alex made him feel. As though he'd been given a new start. There were no smudges yet. No mistakes. Only a wide expanse of white, for as far as he could see. He felt as though he'd been reborn. And this time, he was determined to treat his life, and the lives of those around him, with greater care.

In this isolated place he'd had plenty of time to think. To sort through some of the problems that had plagued him. He still hadn't decided his future. The idea of returning to the force was much less worrisome than it had been earlier. He would take such decisions one day at a time. But for now, he was finally coming to terms with the guilt he'd been suffering over his part in the shoot-out and death. It seemed so easy for Alex to accept the fact that he'd been forced to make a judgment in the space of an instant. Her casual acceptance had caused him to take a hard look at the situation and decide whether he'd been too tough on himself. Right or wrong, he'd concluded, he would have to live with the decision he'd made, and the consequences of it. He'd been forced to take a life in order to try to save one. The fact that both lives had been lost, one his best friend, the other a youth still in his teens, would probably always remain with him. But he was beginning to hope that in time he could let go of the crippling sense of responsibility.

It occurred to him that his nightmare hadn't returned since he'd confided in Alex and had witnessed her calm acceptance of the situation.

Alex. Just looking at her made him smile. The light of excitement in those sparkling eyes. Her cheeks as red as apples. And those long, long legs eating up the miles with so little effort. It may have been her outward beauty that had first attracted him. He'd never met another woman who was his equal in strength and stamina. But it was her inner beauty that had touched his heart and had unlocked all those doors to his emotions. Maybe that was the real reason that he found her so intriguing. She constantly challenged him, mentally and physically. She was, quite simply, the most amazing woman he'd ever met.

They trudged uphill for more than an hour, finally stopping at the ridge to gaze at the serene landscape far below.

"What're those tracks?" Grant pointed and Alex turned to study the line of marks in the snow.

"Deer. At least a dozen I'd say." She bent down, then straightened. "Still fresh. They probably saw us coming and took to those woods. Want to have a look?"

He nodded and left the toboggan resting against a tree to follow her.

As they made their way through the stand of trees, their eyes adjusted to the dim light. The snow wasn't as deep here, and they moved easily into the dense forest. Before long Alex gave a signal to halt. Grant followed her lead and stood perfectly still. Moving toward them was a herd of perhaps a dozen or more deer, with a stag in the lead. As they drew closer the leader paused and sniffed the air. While he stood guard the rest of the herd moved on, passing within feet of Alex and Grant. When the others had moved on, the buck followed, still sniffing the air.

When they were gone, Alex turned to see a look on Grant's face that she recognized. "They got to you, didn't they?"

He nodded. "I'm a city boy. Most of the deer I've seen have been in a zoo. I've never been this close to them in the wild before. I had no idea I'd be so shaken by the experience."

"I know. It catches you by surprise. Even after all these years, I'm still moved each time I see them."

"Then how can you bear to bring hunters here?"

She shrugged. "You'd be surprised to learn that most of the hunters are also conservationists. They realize the necessity of thinning the herds. They're careful and selective. And unless they intend to use the meat themselves, they sign an agreement to donate all the meat to a local food bank. Most of the men who've been coming here for years have switched from rifles to cameras. Their only interest now is in seeing what you and I just saw. It's a fantastic experience.''

Grant nodded. ''It is. Simply amazing.'' He glanced around. ''Think we might see any more wildlife?''

Alex motioned toward the distant ridge of trees. ''I've often spotted a moose in there. Would you like to have a look?''

Grant couldn't hide his eagerness. ''You think it'd be out in broad daylight?''

She shrugged. ''It's hard to say. Some days when I've been up here alone, I've spotted some. But now that the snow has let up, we're more apt to catch sight of a band of them.''

''Why?''

She glanced skyward. ''Because of the snowfall, they're forced to travel farther to forage for food. From the looks of those clouds, we're going to get more snow in the next few days. The animals sense it, and know they have to store up food now so they can settle in until the end of the storm.''

He tugged on a lock of her hair visible beneath the bright yellow cap she'd pulled on. ''How'd you learn all this?''

She smiled. ''I learned a lot from Grandpa Sully. He's always had a great store of knowledge about nature. And from Lem. The rest I've picked up just by living here.''

She suddenly stiffened.

Beside her, Grant went very still. Within minutes a moose moved silently through the woods. The sight of such an animal sent chills along Grant's spine.

The moose was larger than he'd expected, its winter hide thick and shaggy. It moved slowly, taking time to tug on the branches of evergreen.

Grant was so engrossed in what he was seeing, time seemed to stand still. Once, the big bull moose turned its head and stared directly at him and Grant held his breath, afraid he might do something that would cause it to bolt and run. But when the bull turned away, Grant slowly exhaled.

Sometime later the moose began moving, as if by silent command, until it dissolved deeper into the woods and was hidden from view.

"Well. Two sightings in a single day." Alex turned and led the way back to the top of the hill, where they'd left the toboggan. "You must lead a charmed life." She glanced over. "So tell me. Are you getting tired of all this isolation yet?"

He shook his head as he trudged along beside her. "It's funny. I figured a couple of days here and I'd be begging to get back to civilization. Those first few nights I could hardly stand the silence. Now I'm beginning to wonder how I lived all these years without this." He gathered her close. "Or maybe I'm just wondering how I lived all this time without you. You're spoiling me, Alexandra. I may never be able to go back to that other life.''

"That's what happens here.'' She brushed her lips over his. "This place casts a spell over some people, and they're never the same. It's what happened to me the first time I came her with my grandfather. He swears he could see it in my eyes. The rest of my family never understood. Even now they think I'm an odd duck for sticking to the lodge, when I could have my pick of newer, more glamorous hotels anywhere in the world to live.''

He breathed her in, loving the clean fresh fragrance of evergreen that clung to her hair and skin. "I get a rush every time I kiss you.''

"Yeah. I know the feeling.'' She pushed a little away and looked up with an impish grin. "Now you're about to get an even bigger rush.'' She pointed down the long hill, dotted here and there with evergreens. "Are you ready to risk life and limb to ride this toboggan all the way to the bottom?''

His smile was quick and dangerous. "I am if you are.''

"Let's go then.'' She positioned the toboggan, then removed her snowshoes and climbed aboard. "Give me your snowshoes, Grant. You'll have to move fast if you're going to shove off and still get aboard.''

"Don't worry about me, Ms. Sullivan. Just keep an eye out for trees."

He gave the toboggan a hard shove, then leaped aboard and tucked his body tightly against hers. Within minutes they were flying down the hill at breakneck speed, leaning far left, then far right to avoid trees in their path.

The air flew past them, biting their skin like sharp little needles, leaving them breathless.

As they drew near the lake Alex shouted over her shoulder, "Lean left. Hard. Now."

They skimmed across the snow and neatly avoided the shore, heading directly toward the lodge. As they hit flat ground, the toboggan came to a gradual stop.

Grant rolled free and offered a hand to Alex. Both were so exhilarated they could hardly speak.

When he found his voice Grant said, "That was the most fantastic ride of my life. I think it was better than the roller coaster in Atlantic City."

She was laughing. That soft, velvet sound that never failed to touch his heart. "I told you it was a rush."

"Yeah." He kissed her long and hard and deep. When they drew apart he shook his head. "Hmm. I think that was even better. Do you mind if we try that again?"

She was laughing as he dragged her close and kissed her again. Her laughter died as he lingered over her lips until she felt her heart do a series of somersaults.

"Mmm." He drew back slowly, still staring into her eyes. "That's definitely the biggest rush of all." He caught hold of the toboggan rope and started toward the shed. "I'll put this away. And when I come back, I think we'll have to see just how far we can take this."

She was laughing as she started up the steps of the porch. "I can't think of a nicer way to get warm."

"Exactly what I was thinking." Grant was whistling as he strode toward the shed.

Once inside he shook the snow off the toboggan and carefully hung it on a hook. He wouldn't want Lem to find anything out of place.

Grant was still whistling as he made his way to the lodge. As he trudged through the snow it occurred to him that there was a second pair of footprints leading to the porch. Lem must have come to check up on Alex. It was like the old man to see that she was getting by during the storm.

Before going inside Grant stopped by the woodpile and gathered up an armload of logs. What he wanted tonight was a cozy fire, a romantic dinner, and a very long, uninterrupted night of loving. Not necessarily in that order, he thought with a grin.

He nudged the door open with his hip and called, "Honey, I'm home."

When there was no answering response he kicked off his boots, leaving them in the puddle forming beside Alex's. Then he carried the logs into the great room, where he deposited them beside the fireplace. Wiping his hands on his pants he was just turning around when he felt a prickling along his spine.

There were wet footprints across the floor. But how could that be? Alex had shed her boots at the back door. And old Lem was too much of a stickler about neatness to ever walk inside in his boots.

Grant Malone was a man who had always trusted his inner sense. And right now, all his instincts were screaming a warning. Before he had time to react, he heard a sound that had him whirling.

What he saw had his heart stopping.

Alex was in the hallway, standing as still as a statue. A man was standing behind her, his arm wrapped around her throat in a death grip, causing her to struggle for every breath.

As Grant started forward, the man gave a high, shrill laugh and lifted his hand. In it was a very small, very deadly gun, which he very deliberately pressed against Alex's temple. He waited a heartbeat, then pulled the trigger. The click of the empty chamber sounded as thunderous as a cannon in the silence of the room.

"The next one," the man said in that same high, unnaturally shrill tone, "won't be empty. And at this range, I promise you there won't be anything left of this pretty face."

Chapter 14

"Who are you?" Grant kept his tone low, easy, even though his heart was pumping furiously and his years of training had already begun to kick in. The first rule was to keep the shooter talking, until a way could be found to relieve him of his weapon. "What do you want?"

"I'll ask the questions here." The man's voice was jittery with nerves. He waved his gun, then returned it to Alex's temple. "Open your coat. Slowly. Then toss aside your gun."

"I'm not armed." Grant pulled open his parka and eased it to the floor.

"You're lying. I know you better'n that." The voice grew higher, more agitated. "I had plenty of

time to search this place while you were out playing in the snow. There were no weapons in here.
And I know you wouldn't go anywhere without
your gun. So where is it, cop?''

Grant thought about the stash of rifles upstairs,
hidden behind the wall panel, and was thankful for
old Patrick Sullivan's insistence upon secrecy.
Otherwise this madman would have enough artil-
lery to outlast an army. Still, the thought of facing
this intruder without his own gun brought a rush
of frustration. If only he hadn't given in to Alex's
demand.

''What makes you think I'm a cop?''

The intruder's voice rose even higher. ''Don't
play games with me. You're the reason I'm here.
But even if I didn't know who you are, I'd still be
able to tell you're a cop. I can always smell 'em.''

Grant kept his tone level. ''Up here I'm not a
cop. I'm just a tourist.''

''I don't believe you. Once a cop, always a
cop.'' The man tightened his grasp on Alex's
throat. ''You don't want to make me mad, or I'll
have to take it out on your girlfriend here.''

''She's not my…''

''Stop lying.'' The man's eyes were wide, the
pupils glazed.

Grant figured he'd taken a hit of something for
courage. That made him doubly dangerous. He was
not only high, but spoiling for a fight.

"I saw the two of you through the window." The man gave an edgy laugh. "You're so hot for her you practically melted the snow. Now where's your gun?" His eyes narrowed suspiciously as he studied Grant. "Open your shirt."

"I told you..."

He waved the gun wildly. "Shut up and do as I say."

Grant unbuttoned his shirt, all the while gauging the distance between them. The shooter was still too far away to get to. At least not without endangering Alex. He had to get closer. But how?

He pulled apart his unbuttoned shirt. "Satisfied?"

The man shook his head. "Turn around. You could be hiding it behind your back."

Grant complied and turned, lifting his shirt from the waistband of his jeans as he did. "Would you like to come over here and search me?"

"You'd like that wouldn't you, cop? You think I'm dumb enough to let go of your girlfriend here so you can take me on. But I'm wise to all your cop tricks. Take off the shirt."

Grant did as he ordered, letting the flannel shirt drop to the floor. "Now are you satisfied?"

The man nodded. "Okay. You're not packing. That makes it even easier." He visibly relaxed. "Since I'm the only one armed, that makes me king of the hill. And without a weapon to defend yourself, looks like you're out of luck, cop. You're just going to have to dance to my tune."

Grant took a step closer. "What tune is that, punk?"

"Punk, is it? We'll see what you call me before this is over. I came here to see that you paid for my brother's death."

Grant went very still. "Your brother?"

"My name is Vance Kendrick. Brother of Wayne Kendrick." He saw the look of stunned surprise in Grant's eyes, and then the sudden dawning of understanding.

His eyes narrowed. "Yeah. I figured you'd remember that name. You killed him, cop. My baby brother. And I vowed I'd make you pay for that. All the way up here I thought about a dozen different ways to make your dying as slow and painful as possible. My first plan was this."

Without warning he aimed and fired. The bullet slammed into Grant's arm with such force it went clear through, exiting the wound with a river of blood. The force of the bullet drove Grant against the wall, where he dropped to his knees, pressing a hand to his flesh to stem the bleeding. But it was useless to try. Blood streamed between his fingers, staining his chest and the front of his jeans.

"No! Grant! No!" Horrified, Alex cried out and tried to break free of the arms that held her. But it was useless. The gunman simply tightened his grasp until she could no longer breathe. Before she slipped into unconsciousness, he loosened his hold enough to allow a few struggling breaths. And all the while he laughed.

"Yeah, cop. That was my first plan. To just shoot you and keep on shooting until you begged me to kill you to put you out of your misery. But it wasn't until I watched you through that window that it came to me. The best possible way to even the score." He rubbed the pistol against Alex's cheek like a caress and laughed when she flinched. "Now that I've seen the way it is between you and the pretty lady, I figure the best way to hurt you is to hurt her. And make you watch."

Grant's hands clenched in impotent fury. "Leave her out of this. She had nothing to do with what happened to your brother."

"But you did, cop. You're the one who pulled the trigger and blew him away. And now it's pay-day. You took the life of someone I cared for. Now it's my turn to do the same to you."

"All right." Despite the almost blinding pain, Grant forced himself to stand, leaning against the wall for support. "Here I am. Take your best shot."

"Just like that?"

Grant nodded. "Why not? What you have in mind can't be any worse than what I've already gone through. Do you think I like knowing I killed a kid? If you shoot me, you'll just be putting me out of my misery."

"Aw, you're breaking my heart. But I still say hurting the woman is the best way to get to you."

Grant could feel himself fading in and out, and was desperate to end this before he lost consciousness completely. His voice lowered, to soothe, to coax. "If you leave now, I won't be able to follow you."

"Leave?" Vance roared with laughter. "Do you know how hard it was to find you? When I finally discovered where you were staying, it took me three stolen cars to get this far. Then I got caught in a snowstorm, and had to abandon the last car a couple of miles from here. I walked through waist-high drifts just to find you, cop."

"Then think about this." Grant struggled to keep the edge of pain and shock from seeping into his voice. "If you give yourself up, you'll face nothing more than a simple breaking-and-entering, along with car theft. But if you go through with your plan, you'll have every police force from here to New York searching for a cop killer."

Vance shook his head, still laughing. "I know your kind. You're all alike. You think you can talk me into setting down this gun and letting you put the cuffs on me. You're going to spout that garbage about this being a simple case as long as I don't kill someone. You'll go easy on me if I let your girlfriend go. And you'll put in a good word with the judge if I give in peacefully." He gave a high, shrill laugh that scraped across their already taut nerves. "Think again, cop. I have no intention of going easy on you and the woman. There isn't a judge in this country who'd let me do simple time. Not after they looked into my record and found out about the stolen car ring, and the number of carjackings I've been involved in, and the street thugs I've had to take out in order to be number one."

"How many people do you think have died because of you?" Grant didn't expect an answer, but he was determined to keep this wild man talking while he tried to figure how to get Alex safely away from him.

To his surprise, Vance stood a little straighter and boasted, "More than you can claim, cop."

"What does that mean?"

"There've been dozens. At least half of them were women and girls, and I showed them a real good time before I finally killed them."

Grant saw the look of revulsion on Alex's face, and wished he could spare her. But he realized this madman craved this opportunity to brag. Seeing this as the perfect chance to distract him, he shook his head in denial. "You're lying."

"Am I?" Vance dragged Alex firmly against him and leaned close enough to press his mouth to her temple. "I'll let your girlfriend here have a chance to find out in just a few minutes. And all you'll be able to do is watch, cop."

Alex was filled with such dread, she feared at any moment her legs might buckle. Still, she stood as still as a statue, hoping to hold her fear at bay, for Grant's sake.

Grant. The sight of blood streaming down his arm, smearing his chest, had tears very close to the surface. She blinked them back furiously. There was no time for tears now. She had to find a way to save the man she loved.

"Tell me about the ones you killed." Grant gritted his teeth against the pain and tried to concentrate. There had to be a way to save Alex. As for himself, it no longer mattered. He would die a happy man if he could know that she was safely away from this monster.

"You really want to know?"

"Yeah." Grant took a deep breath and watched Vance's eyes.

"There was the old man and woman who thought they could stop me from taking their brand new van. It was on the top of my wish list. I told the old guy not to try to be a hero, but he wouldn't listen. After I shot him, the old woman picked up a cell phone. So I had to stop her, too. I figured, before I shot her, I might as well have a little fun for myself."

He enjoyed the hiss of disgust that issued from
Alex's lips. He grinned, enjoying himself. "Then
there was the Red Shirt who wanted the same car
I wanted."

Grant glanced at Alex, hoping the sound of his
voice would give her the strength she needed to
get through this. "Red Shirts are members of a
rival street gang. Vance and his brother were members of another gang we'd been watching for
months."

Vance gave a sneer. "The Red Shirts are nothing but two-bit punks. They can't even shoot
straight. After I had my fun with his lady, I took
him out with a single shot."

Alex closed her eyes, trying to blot out the images his words had planted in her mind. The horror
of what he'd done, without a trace of remorse, had
tears clouding her vision.

He grinned. "So you see, cop? You're not the
only one who knows how to use a gun." He waved
his weapon proudly. "This gun has seen a lot more
death than yours. The only difference between us
is that you get paid to kill guys like me. And when
you do, you're called a hero. The Manhattan
Hero." His tone grew more shrill. "You think that
badge makes you better'n the rest of us. But you
weren't better'n Wayne. You just got in a lucky
shot. In a fair fight, he'd have beat you hands
down."

Grant froze. The mere mention of that boy's name still had a chilling effect on him. "And how would you know that?"

"Because I taught him myself. Everything I could. How to take cover. How to draw a bead on a moving target. How to make every bullet count."

Grant's voice lowered with disbelief. "You taught your own brother how to kill?"

"On the streets it's kill or be killed."

"He didn't have to be on the streets. It was after two in the morning. He was just a kid. He should have been home in bed."

"Wayne had a job to do. The same as me. We had a list of cars to deliver. If we got them all in on time, we earned a bonus. Wayne knew I wanted that bonus. He was working overtime to see that I got it, so that I'd give him a piece of it."

For the first time Alex managed to speak over the sense of horror that clogged her throat. "So you're the reason your brother died."

"Why you…" Furious, Vance tugged viciously on her hair, drawing her head back in a painful grip. He pressed the muzzle of his gun to her temple while he hissed out a breath. "Your boyfriend there is the only reason my brother is dead."

"You can tell yourself that." Alex saw the look of frustration on Grant's face, and knew that he was silently pleading with her to remain quiet. Still, the anger inside her exploded. She thought

about all the months Grant had agonized over the
shooting. The doctors. The pills. The sleepless
nights he lay awake blaming himself. While this
man had spent the entire time blaming others and
plotting revenge. "But you know better. If you
hadn't given your brother a gun and sent him out
on the street, he'd still be alive."

Enraged, he gripped her by both shoulders and
turned her to face him. "Why you…"

She refused to back down. Instead she lifted her
chin and faced him. "It wasn't a police officer who
killed your brother. It was you."

"Shut up." He brought the pistol down against
the side of her temple, drawing blood.

Grant was nearly blinded by fury. It swirled like
a red mist before his eyes. He saw Vance take aim
and knew, without a doubt, that Alex had no
chance against this madman. He charged across the
room, his only thought to take the bullet meant for
Alex. As he leapt, he heard the terrible, deafening
sound of an explosion.

He saw the look of shock and pain on Alex's
face as the color slowly drained away. Saw the
ever-widening spill of blood staining the front of
her sweater. Reflexively his hand shot out. In one
smooth movement he shoved her aside and sent
her tumbling to the floor. Then his hand was at
Vance's throat in an iron grip, pressing so hard the
gunman could feel his life beginning to ebb. With

a grunt Vance released his hold on the gun in an effort to pry the offending hand loose. But Grant couldn't be budged. Blinded by pain and rage, he was determined to take the life of the man who had cost Alex hers.

Grant continued to choke him until Vance brought a knee to his groin, sending him to the floor, doubled over in pain. In the blink of an eye Vance was on him, a snarling, raging avenger, pinning him down while pressing the gun to his forehead.

Grant's voice was so cold, so controlled, it was barely recognizable. "Go ahead, punk. With the woman I love dead, my life isn't worth living anyway. You'll be doing me a favor by killing me."

The gunman threw back his head and laughed. "Oh, this is worth all the days and nights I spent planning my revenge. I love it. A cop begging me to end his life. And believe me, I'm more than willing to do as you ask."

As he took aim, he suddenly stiffened, then went limp and fell forward. Grant blinked, unable to believe his eyes. Standing over him was Alex, holding a log from the hearth.

"You're not dead?" Grant rolled to one side, then got stiffly to his knees and touched a hand to hers. "Oh, baby, you're not dead."

She gave a shaky laugh. "I guess not. But I've

got an awful pain in my arm. I think the bullet went clean through.''

''Oh, thank God.'' He gathered her close for a minute, needing to touch her, to hold her.

He looked over when Vance moaned and started to sit up. Grabbing up the pistol, Grant knelt over him and pointed the gun at his chest. ''Now what're you going to do, punk?''

''Don't…shoot.'' With his throat bruised and swollen, the words were little more than a croak.

''Why not? It's what you intended to do to us. Why should I be better than you?''

Alex clapped a hand over her mouth to keep from crying out. With silent tears streaming down her face she touched a hand to Grant's shoulder. She was shocked to feel the tension humming through him. A tension so terrible, his whole body vibrated with it.

She understood his need to avenge this horror. She shared that need. But not with a gun, she realized.

''Please don't kill him, Grant.'' Her voice lowered to a whisper. ''If you do, he'll win. Don't you see? You just asked why you should be better. The reason is simple. You're a cop. All your life, that's all you wanted to be. Because your grandfather was. Because you wanted to cheer for the good guys and stop the bad guys. It was something you did with pride. Don't let him rob you of that pride now.''

She studied the wide, fearful eyes of the man staring at the gun. And then she saw the icy, narrowed gaze of the one holding that gun. There was such anger in Grant. Such barely controlled fury. She prayed she could find a way to diffuse that hatred before he did something he'd regret for a lifetime.

''You've been given a second chance, Grant. And this time you can make it all right.''

She held her breath while Grant continued studying the man through narrowed eyes. Then, as he slowly got to his feet, she felt her heart begin to beat again.

His words were terse, spat from between tightly clenched teeth. ''Are you strong enough to phone the sheriff?''

She nodded through her tears.

He dragged her close, needing to feel her warmth, her spirit, her life. Against her hair he muttered, ''Tell him we're holding a fugitive at the lodge.'' He took a deep breath and added, ''Tell him to hurry. I wouldn't want anything to happen to this punk until he's had a chance to pay his debt to society.''

Chapter 15

The lodge had become a scene of absolute bedlam. The sheriff and his deputy from the little town of Snug Harbor arrived behind the town's only snowplow. Trailing them was a car bearing a doctor and nurse from the town's clinic, who had been notified of gunshot wounds. Bringing up the rear of the convoy was a truck with a reporter and a photographer from the local *Gazette*. Lem, who had been alerted by the sheriff, arrived by snowmobile at the same time that Bren and her daughters came roaring up in their van.

On his way to the lodge the sheriff had contacted the authorities in New York, who arrived within hours in three helicopters, now cluttering the surface of the frozen lake.

Inside, lawmen kept a silent watch over the prisoner, while the local sheriff, along with the state police, tried to conduct interviews with both Alex and Grant, after they had been treated by the doctor and nurse. And all the while, the reporter and photographer roamed the lodge, snapping pictures, interviewing everyone who could add to their store of information.

Through it all, Bren and her daughters brewed gallons of coffee and passed out sandwiches to grateful police officers. When they weren't handling food and drinks they were mopping up bloodstains from the floors and walls, and marveling that no deaths had occurred with so much blood spilled. In fact, the doctor had found, to his amazement, that the bullets had done no serious damage as they had passed through limbs. Grant's was by far the more serious of the two, though he refused treatment until the doctor confirmed that Alex had suffered nothing but a simple flesh wound.

Despite the fact that Grant was familiar with the routine, it was evident that his patience with his fellow police officers was wearing thin with each succeeding hour.

Finally, seeing the pallor of Alex's face, his fury exploded. He glowered at the police chief. "We've already answered your questions, Chief Miller.

Anything else you want answered will have to wait.''

He picked Alex up, cradling her against his chest. ''What Miss Sullivan needs now is a sedative and some time to rest.''

''But Grant...'' Her protest was cut off as he shoved past a line of cops and stormed down the hall to her bedroom.

Inside, Bren already had the bedding turned down and a fire burning on the hearth. On the night table was a steaming cup of herbal tea and one of the doctor's strongest sedatives. Chopin was playing softly on a CD.

Grant settled Alex gently in the bed and handed her the tablet, followed by a sip of water. He waited until she'd swallowed the sedative before turning to Bren. ''You'll stay and take care of her?''

''Of course.''

''Where are you going?'' Alex reached for his hand.

He paused to press it between both of his. ''I'll have to fly back with the prisoner and file a complete report.''

''To New York?''

He nodded. ''A couple of state police offered to drive my Jeep back.''

''Your Jeep?'' Her heart took a hard, solid jolt. ''Aren't you planning on coming back?''

He hesitated before saying softly, "I love you, Alexandra. I always will. But I realized something today. It isn't enough to love someone. Not if it means that by loving them, you place them in harm's way."

"Grant..."

He shook his head. "There's no denying what I've done. If Vance Kendrick hadn't so easily read my feelings for you, you could have been spared all this pain and anxiety. It's because of me that you had to suffer. How many people should have to suffer because of me? Jason is dead; my sister is now a widow with a child to raise alone. And you're suffering the effects of a madman bent on revenge. Your precious privacy has been violated, your secluded hideaway invaded. And all because of me. Lem was right. You're too tenderhearted for your own good. And once again you're the one who has to bear the scars for your goodness."

He leaned down, oblivious to the fact that Bren was watching them. With a sigh of frustration he brushed his lips over hers. Then, feeling the tremors she couldn't hide, he took the kiss deeper. "Try not to think about what happened here. Just get some rest."

"What about you, Grant? When do you get to rest?"

He gave her a weak smile. "This is my job. Remember?"

He squeezed her fingers, then lifted them to his lips for a quick kiss before striding quickly across the room.

With his hand on the knob he turned. The sight of her bloodstained dressings had a muscle working in his jaw. His eyes were every bit as fierce as the first time she'd seen him. The seething anger in him frightened her.

"I have…a lot of things to deal with, Alex. But know that I love you." Without giving her a chance to speak he pulled the door shut behind him.

Alex closed her eyes and listened to the sound of his footsteps receding along the hall. Then, with a sigh catching in her throat, she gave in and allowed Bren to help her out of her bloody clothes.

Alex lay in her bed and listened to the sounds of silence that had finally settled over the lodge. She'd begun to think that all the people who'd invaded her privacy might never leave. But now, after convincing Bren that she truly wanted to be alone, she had her wish.

Bren had taken her girls home to bed, but only after extracting a promise from Alex that she would phone whenever she was awake and in need of her.

The sedative old Dr. McBride had given her left her brain fogged and her body sluggish. She knew

she'd slept through the night and the better part of
the day. She'd awakened once or twice through the
night to glance at the midnight sky outside her window. She'd seen the morning light filtering through
her bedroom, before she'd drifted to sleep again.
Now the sun had made its arc across the sky and
would soon be setting.

Grant hadn't phoned.

She knew he wasn't going to return. The depth
of his self-loathing, and the fierceness of his dec-
laration of love had said it all. He was once again
blaming himself for everything that had happened.
And this time she was helpless to change his mind.

She would have to settle for the fact that he had
achieved what he'd come seeking at Snug Harbor
Lodge. His night terrors had disappeared. His self-
esteem had been restored. Strangely enough, it had
been his young victim's own brother who had
given Grant his final peace of mind. If Vance
hadn't admitted teaching Wayne how to use a gun
to kill efficiently, Grant would still be blaming
himself for that boy's death. Now, finally, he could
accept that Wayne Kendrick had been, regardless
of his tender age, an accomplished gunman.

She was happy for Grant. And relieved that his
wish had been granted. But she also knew that he
now had no reason to return. He was, after all,
confident enough to look to his future. A future
that lay in the city. Doing what he'd always wanted

to do. And now, finally, he could return with a sense of pride and accomplishment.

Still, though she loved him, she couldn't imagine her life anywhere but here. Not even for the man she loved.

The man she loved. How had all this happened? How had she been foolish enough to allow such feelings for a man who was all wrong for her? He was city born and bred. That same city held his future. While hers was tied to this wilderness.

Agitated, she tossed and turned, rolling from side to side until, exhausted, she drifted back into a restless sleep.

The snowstorm Alex had predicted had finally arrived in all its fury. Snowflakes beat angrily against the windowpane and formed a thick curtain that nearly obliterated everything beyond the porch.

Bren stood at the stove stirring a pot of soup. She turned when Alex entered the kitchen.

"Any calls, Bren?"

"Grant phoned half a dozen times yesterday. He said not to wake you. He just wanted to be sure that you were being properly taken care of."

"He didn't ask to speak with me?"

Bren saw the expectant look in her young friend's eyes and felt a wave of sadness as she shook her head.

Seeing Alex easing into a parka she gave a look of alarm. "Where are you going?"

"Just down to the lake. I need to get outdoors for a while."

"Alex…"

"I'm fine now, Bren. Even Dr. McBride said so when he checked me this morning. I won't be long." She managed a smile before stepping onto the porch and pulling the door shut behind her.

Once she was out of sight, the smile faded. Grant hadn't wanted to speak with her. It could only mean that he wasn't coming back.

What would she do if he never came back?

She paused on the banks of the lake and stared around at the snow-covered vastness of her surroundings. Finding a fallen log she sat, deep in thought. Despite the pain in her heart, she knew what she would do. What she'd always done. She would go on living and working here. She would invest her energy in her guests. In her friends and family. In herself and nature and all the things she'd always loved. She would endure. She would survive. She sighed. She would go on. Perhaps not as happily or as innocently as before. But she would survive.

A short time later she made her way back toward the lodge. As she started past the two snowpeople, she paused to study their linked fingers. The sight of it caused such a pain around her heart, she was forced to close her eyes. She might endure, she reminded herself, but she would never again love anyone the way she'd loved Grant Malone.

It wasn't so much a sound as a sense of someone behind her that caused her to turn. Grant was standing there, watching her with that same intense expression she'd come to know so well.

Her tone was too breathy, but she couldn't seem to help it. "I've been worried about you."

"Yeah." He stayed where he was, afraid to touch her. Afraid if he did, she'd vanish like the mist over the lake.

In the week he'd been away, he could see in his mind the bloodred stains that had marred Alex's flesh. His hands clenched at his sides. It had nearly torn out his heart to see her hurt like that. In that moment, he'd known a blood-lust that had nearly sent him over the edge of reason. To see the woman he loved taking a bullet because of him had caused a pain unlike any he'd ever known.

The woman he loved. He studied her eyes, rimmed with fatigue. And her skin, a bit too pale. His fault, he thought. All his fault.

"You came to say goodbye, didn't you?" She could see it in his eyes. In the tightness of his mouth.

"Alexandra…"

She closed her eyes and turned away to hide the tears. "I understand. Your future is in New York.

And now that you've come to terms with what happened between you and Wayne Kendrick, you'll be able to get back to the work you love.''

''It's funny.'' His voice, so close behind her, sent a chill along her spine. ''I came up here honestly believing that I'd never again be able to function as a good cop. I'd pretty much resigned myself to that fact. And then, when I met you, and realized just how sweet your life was here at Snug Harbor, I started to think about a future here with you.''

When she glanced over her shoulder he caught her arched brow and gave a bitter laugh. ''Yeah. How about that? A city boy thinking about making it in the wilderness. But then I wondered what I'd do. I could never earn a living as a trail guide. The only thing I know how to do well is police work.''

''So you've decided to go back to the city.''

His voice lowered. ''I'd say that's pretty much up to you.''

She turned. ''I don't understand.''

For a moment longer he didn't speak. He merely stared at her, drinking in the way she looked. She was wearing a simple parka. Her hair hung soft and loose around a face free of makeup. He'd never seen anyone look so vulnerable or so beautiful. Quite simply, every time he looked at her she took his breath away.

She felt a quick flutter of fear as the silence

stretched out. "Do you want to go back to the force?"

He shrugged. "When the chief made it plain that my old job is still waiting, I found myself thinking I was ready. But are you, Alexandra? Would you be able to live with a husband who was a cop?"

"I could never live in New York."

"I know. I'd never ask that of you. But there's been another offer. One I'm considering. I just left Snug Harbor, where I met with Chief Miller. He's offered me a job."

"A job?" She looked puzzled. "He already has a deputy. Billy Winters."

"Yeah. He says Winters is a good cop. He thinks I'd like working with him."

"Does he think a little town like Snug Harbor needs two deputies?"

"He's offered me the job of chief. It turns out that Chief Miller is retiring in the spring. He talked to my superiors while they were here, and they've already faxed him a copy of my records. He'd like me to consider stepping in as his replacement."

For a moment Alex was afraid to speak. If she did, he'd hear the note of eager expectancy in her voice. Or worse, a note of pleading. Finally, after a deep breath she managed to say, "You're a good cop, Grant. Your fellow officers consider you one of the best."

"Being a good cop isn't enough, Alex. There's

no denying that if I hadn't been here, none of this would have happened to you. It's because of me that you had to suffer at the hands of that punk. There could be another one some day, looking for revenge.''

That look was back in his eyes. That hot, fierce look of self-loathing she'd come to recognize. She turned away and lifted her head to the falling snow.

With her back to him she said softly, "It's a funny thing about storms. They come blowing in with no regard to the destruction they cause. Roads are closed. Power gets knocked out. And then the good guys come along, and plow the roads, and repair the electrical wires. And in no time we forget all about the storm, and concentrate on the beauty it left behind.''

Puzzled, he stepped closer, reluctant to touch her. If he did touch her, he'd crush her against him, and cause her more pain. Instead, he satisfied himself with a mere touch of her hair. "Are you saying Vance Kendrick was nothing more than a wayward storm?''

She nodded. "Sometimes such things are planned. Other times, they seem to be simple acts of random violence. Either way, the victims are always grateful for the men who are trained to clean up the destruction.''

He watched the way the strands of honey hair sifted through his fingers. "I feel as though I vi-

olated the beauty of your wilderness. That some-
how it'll never be the same because of me.''

"In one way it won't be. The Native Americans
who once lived here believed that each person who
passes through leaves a part of himself behind. But
think about this." She pointed to the swirling
snowflakes. "By morning the tracks of the trucks
and snowmobiles and helicopters will all be obliterated."

"You think so?"

She nodded. "You won't even be able to tell
anyone was here." She turned and drew his face
down for a soft, tentative kiss.

At once they both felt the rush of heat and took
the kiss deeper.

"You're sure?" he whispered against her
mouth. "You're sure that in time all the…tracks
will be obliterated, and the beauty of this place will
be unharmed if I stay?"

"Oh, my darling, I've never been so sure of anything in my life."

"I was so afraid. So afraid on the drive here that
you'd never be able to forgive me for the destruction I brought."

"You didn't bring it, Grant. It just blew in like
a storm. And now it's gone."

He took a deep breath. "I don't want to just stay
here with you, Alex. If I stay, I want it to be per-
manent." He glanced down at their linked fingers,

and then at the two snowpeople, who were slowly being covered with a fresh layer of clean, white powder. "I'm talking marriage. And forever."

"Forever." She sighed, then whispered, "I'm not sure that's going to be long enough."

He laughed and lifted her gently into his arms. She fit so perfectly against him, like the missing piece of a puzzle. He lowered his face to her hair and breathed her in before heading toward the lodge. Halfway there he paused to kiss her again. "You're right. That isn't nearly long enough. I won't settle for anything less than eternity."

"I'm willing if you are." She wrapped her arms around his neck, feeling all the warmth of love flowing between them.

As their lips met, she reminded herself that she'd have to phone Grandpa Sully and thank him for this, the most beautiful, wonderful gift he'd ever sent her.

The gift of love.

Epilogue

"Hold still, Alex, or I'm never going to get you dressed." Lizbeth Sullivan stood in Alex's bedroom, helping her into her gown. Her blond hair had already slipped from its neat pins to frizz around her cheeks. She wore an ankle-length dress of palest peach which, at the moment, matched the pink of her glowing cheeks. "Why do they make so many of these tiny fasteners on wedding gowns?"

"To frustrate the poor groom who has to deal with them later." Celeste Sullivan, looking sleek and sophisticated in a bronze Armani cocktail suit, her red, chin-length hair pulled behind one ear with a jeweled comb, stepped inside and closed the door behind her. "I just had a look at your husband-to-be. He is, to quote Kayla and Kelsey, some kind of hunk."

Lizbeth looked up. "Well? What did you expect?"

"To be honest, I wasn't sure just what to expect. He is, after all, marrying our Alex. I thought he'd be a cross between a Marine drill sergeant and some sort of nature nerd."

"Thanks, Celeste." Alex was too happy to take the bait. "As far as I know he doesn't spit bullets or eat worms. And he hasn't asked me to live in a cave."

"That's a comfort." Celeste bent over the night table to inhale the perfume of a bouquet of white roses. "These are fabulous. Who sent them?"

"My drill sergeant." Alex watched her sister's face in the mirror as she read the note that accompanied them.

"Oh." Celeste touched a hand to her heart. "The man not only looks like a Greek god, he has the heart of a poet as well." Just then Alex turned and she was nearly overcome with tears. "Oh, Alex. You look so beautiful."

The three sisters embraced, then Lizbeth and Celeste stepped back, smoothing the wrinkles from the long column of snow-white silk that adorned their oldest sister.

"I'm so happy for you, Alex." Lizbeth dabbed a lace handkerchief to her eyes.

"Me, too." Celeste heard the crunch of tires in the snow and looked up. "That'll be Reverend Hawkins."

At the door she turned. "I hope you like what I did with the great room."

Alex's eyes glittered with laughter. "Lizbeth told me the local florist almost quit after you began redoing all his arrangements."

"I told him this was a wedding, for heaven's sake, not the local bridge club's annual tea. I sent him back to his shop for the biggest baskets he could find, and had him fill them with masses of holiday flowers. Now the room looks worthy of a Sullivan celebration."

When she flounced out, Alex and Lizbeth waited until the door closed before bursting into gales of laughter.

Alex shook her head. "Why am I not surprised?"

Lizbeth chuckled. "Leave it to Celeste. But the truth is, Alex, she has an excellent eye. You're going to love what she did."

"You mean I won't find myself surrounded by crystal swans?"

They shared another laugh before Lizbeth shook her head. "It looks…simply perfect." She turned toward the door. "Speaking of perfect, I promised

Bren I'd help her in the kitchen. I brought a few of my specialties along for the wedding supper."

Alex laughed. "Knowing you, it's probably more like a dozen specialties."

"Well…more or less. You know how I love to cook." Smiling, Lizbeth hurried away, just as her parents stepped into Alex's room for a few minutes alone with their daughter before the ceremony began.

"Told you we'd find Grant in here hiding from all your noisy relations, Sully."

Grant turned from the window to see his grandfather stepping into his room, followed by Patrick Sullivan, carrying a bottle of fine Irish whiskey and three tumblers.

When Sully finished pouring he handed one to Mickey Finn and one to Grant.

"Look at you, boy." Mickey beamed with pride. "The new police chief of Snug Harbor, New Hampshire."

"Police chief-in-training. It won't be official until spring."

"You already look like the man in charge, doesn't he, Sully?"

"That he does, Mickey." Sully fixed him with a look. "I hope you realize what a special woman you're about to wed. Ever since she was just a wee lass that one's owned my heart."

"I do know, sir. And I'm grateful every day that you and my grandfather persuaded me to come up here."

"We had an idea this place might be just the thing you needed." Mickey's eyes glinted with humor. "Of course, it didn't hurt that Alex was part of the package."

Grant kept his eyes steady on his grandfather's. "You old schemer."

"It worked, didn't it?" He lifted his tumbler. "Here's to the lass who mended your heart. And then stole it clean away."

Laughing, the three men drank.

"I remember telling Sully fifteen or twenty years ago that I had a handsome young grandson who ought to suit at least one of his pretty little granddaughters."

"These things take time." Sully filled their tumblers a second time, then lifted his glass. "Here's to time. May it bring you all the things your heart desires."

Grant drank.

Mickey clapped his old friend on the shoulder. "Speaking of time, do you remember the time we bet a hundred dollars on which of us would get the first catch of the season?"

Grant set his tumbler down and started toward the door.

"Here now." Mickey called after him. "I was

just getting started on a grand story. Where do you think you're going?''

''To find my heart's desire.''

The two old men watched as he stalked out of the room, slamming the door behind him.

Sully threw back his head and roared. ''Looks like even your own grandson doesn't want to hear about any more of your tired old bets.''

''Tired, are they? Well, here's a new one.'' Mickey reached into his pocket and slammed a hundred dollars down on the night table. ''This bill says those prim and proper granddaughters of yours will do everything in their power to stop him from seeing the bride.''

''Ah. But will they succeed?'' Sully was already reaching into his pocket to match the bet.

''Not a chance. He's my grandson, after all.''

''I agree. Those two will never let tradition get in the way. If my Alex wants to kiss her groom before the ceremony, I'm betting she'll do it. And nobody will stop her. So we've nothing to bet on.''

''Nothing to bet on?''

At Mickey's words, the two old men looked suddenly deflated until he said, ''We could always bet on how soon we'll have our first great-grandchild.''

Sully's eyes lit with fire as he mentally counted the months. ''I'm betting by this time next Christmas.''

"You're on. I'm saying it'll be sooner. October or November."

The two men shook hands, then proceeded to pour another tumbler.

Sully's smile was as bright as the sunshine reflecting off the snow outside the window. "We made a good match, Mickey."

"That we did, my friend."

Alex kissed her mother and father and watched them rejoin the guests in the great room. No sooner had she closed the door when there was a soft tap.

She opened the door to find Grant's sister in the doorway. In her arms was her infant son. She and her parents, along with dozens of Alex's relatives, had spent the past weekend at the lodge, getting acquainted. They had come together as strangers, but had quickly become friends.

"Come in, Ellen."

"Only for a minute. I just wanted to tell you that when Grant first told us he was leaving New York to settle down here in Snug Harbor, I thought he was making a terrible mistake."

"And now?"

"I envy him. I really like the town. And this lodge is so peaceful." She glanced at the infant asleep in her arms. "I'm beginning to think I'd like Jason to grow up in a place like this."

Alex smiled. "You'd like it here, Ellen. There's

a really nice school in town. They're probably in need of a good teacher.'' She opened her arms. ''May I?''

''He might drool on your gown.''

''I wouldn't mind a little baby drool.'' Alex lifted the blanket-clad baby from Ellen's arms and brushed a kiss over his soft, downy cheek. ''Oh, he smells so wonderful.''

Just then Grant came stalking into her room, his eyes looking as hot and fierce as the first time she'd seen him.

At the sight of her holding his nephew he came to a halt and felt a sudden burning in his throat.

She looked at him with a smile that would melt mountains of snow. ''Ellen is thinking she might like to raise little Jason right here in Snug Harbor. Wouldn't that be nice? I'm sure she could get a job teaching at the school.''

''Yeah. And just think. You'll have the inside track with the chief of police.'' He continued to stare at Alex. ''You look pretty natural holding that baby.''

''Do I?'' She could feel the heat of his look clear across the room.

''Well…'' Ellen glanced from one to the other, then reached out and took her son from Alex's arms. ''I think I hear the music starting.''

''We'll be along. In a minute.'' Grant waited until she closed the door before stepping closer.

Just then there was another sharp rap and the door was opened. With a snarl Grant stepped back and turned to see Lem standing in the doorway.

"Sorry." The old man hesitated.

"Lem." Alex hurried over to catch his hands and draw him inside.

"I know they're all waiting out there. But I wanted to say my piece before you two get swallowed up by the crowd." He glanced at Grant. "I'm sorry I meddled."

"You didn't meddle, Lem." Grant placed a hand on the old man's arm. "You were looking out for Alexandra. And you had every right. I came here with a chip on my shoulder and a demon in my soul."

The old man smiled. "Looks to me like you're a man at peace with himself now."

Grant nodded.

Lem turned to Alex. "I never had a daughter. But if I did, I'd want her to be just like you."

She felt tears spring to her eyes as she leaned close to kiss his cheek. "You've been my best friend, Lem. I hope you'll continue to be."

"You know I will, Alex." Looking slightly flustered, he offered his hand to Grant. "I know you'll take good care of her."

Grant accepted his handshake. "I'd better. Because you'll still be here every day, I hope. Seeing that I do."

"You can count on it." The old man walked to the door. "Now you two had better get out there. You've got a lot of people eager to share your happiness."

"We'll be right there," Alex murmured as she closed the door.

Grant started toward her. "Not just yet."

She gathered up her nosegay of white rosebuds and turned toward him. "We can't hold up the ceremony."

"Why can't we?"

"Because...all those people are waiting." She touched a hand to his cheek. "You look... worried."

He shook his head. "Not worried. Thunder-struck. Do you realize this is the first time I've ever seen you in a dress?"

"Really?" Pleased, she turned a complete circle, allowing the silk to whisper around her ankles. "What do you think?"

"It's perfect. You're perfect. I still don't know how this happened. I feel like the luckiest man in the world."

"You are. And I'll spend the rest of my life reminding you of that fact."

He caught her hand and lifted it to his lips. "Promise?"

She felt the rush of heat all the way to her toes. Would it always be like this? she wondered. Would he always have the power to make her weak with a single touch?

"We'd better go. The music has been playing for a full minute now, and the crowd will be getting restless."

"Wait." He drew her back and brushed his mouth over hers. "Out there, with everyone watching, I may forget a few lines. But know this. I love you, Alexandra Sullivan. And I'm so grateful to you for saving my life."

"Maybe we saved each other's."

"Maybe we did." He linked his fingers with hers, before opening the door and starting down the hall.

She moved along beside him, achingly aware that they were about to change their lives forever.

Forever.

She glanced at her Grandpa Sully, wiping a tear from his eyes. And saw her parents and sisters wearing matching looks of pride and joy.

Her relatives and friends, standing in a sea of flowers that had been artfully arranged in huge baskets, were smiling. Kayla and Kelsey, who had been thrilled when she'd asked them to act as junior bridesmaids, were blushing and giggling.

And then the crowd faded from view as she turned to Grant. All she could see was the love in those fierce, dark eyes. All she could hear was his voice, low and deep as he spoke his vows. All she could feel were his strong arms as he drew her close for a kiss. This was, she knew, all she would ever want or need.

She'd taken in a wounded stranger, and had found the greatest treasure of all—the love of a lifetime. She no longer had to wonder whether or not a city cop could find true love with a free spirit whose home was in the wilderness.

Life, she thought with a sigh as Grant took the kiss deeper, was a lot like the New Hampshire wilderness. There seemed to be a wonderful surprise around every bend in the trail.

* * * * *

Read about the man who steals Lizbeth Sullivan's heart in

LOVING LIZBETH.

Look for it next month only in Silhouette Sensation®.

2 Books
and a surprise gift!

We would like to take this opportunity to thank you for reading this Silhouette® book by offering you the chance to take TWO more specially selected titles from the Sensation™ series absolutely FREE! We're also making this offer to introduce you to the benefits of the Reader Service™ —

- ★ FREE home delivery
- ★ FREE gifts and competitions
- ★ FREE monthly Newsletter
- ★ Books available before they're in the shops
- ★ Exclusive Reader Service discounts

Accepting these FREE books and gift places you under no obligation to buy; you may cancel at any time, even after receiving your free shipment. Simply complete your details below and return the entire page to the address below. **You don't even need a stamp!**

YES! Please send me 2 free Sensation books and a surprise gift. I understand that unless you hear from me, I will receive 4 superb new titles every month for just £2.80 each, postage and packing free. I am under no obligation to purchase any books and may cancel my subscription at any time. The free books and gift will be mine to keep in any case.

S1ZEB

Ms/Mrs/Miss/Mr ....Initials ....
BLOCK CAPITALS PLEASE

Surname ....

Address ....

....

....Postcode ....

Send this whole page to:
UK: The Reader Service, FREEPOST CN81, Croydon, CR9 3WZ
EIRE: The Reader Service, PO Box 4546, Kilcock, County Kildare (stamp required)